THE WORLD BREAKER REQUIEM

ALSO BY LUKE TARZIAN

SHADOW TWINS

Vultures

House of Muir (Forthcoming)

ADJACENT MONSTERS

The World Maker Parable

ANTHOLOGIES

Dark Ends

THE WORLD BREAKER REQUIEM

AN ADJACENT MONSTERS NIGHTMARE

LUKE TARZIAN

LT
DOT
COM

To mothers taken far too soon

and children feeling lost.

ARIATH

HELVEDEN

THE RUIN
OF ULM

THE PEA

GIL'AN
MOR

NIL-IL

OLD JÉMOON

BANEROWOS

YLL

THE SONJA OCEAN

OF DREN

RACH
NA'SCHUUL

"But the stars that marked our starting fall away. We must go deeper into greater pain, for it is not permitted that we stay."

— Dante Alighieri, *The Inferno*

Prologue—Rach Na'Schuul

I am timeless, though my soul has felt the wax and wane of millennia as I watch realities rise and fall.

The stars shine high above my city Rach Na'Schuul as they have done for years; memories and hopes, for my beloved home is dead, cast to ruin by the god-things of Jémoon. By the madness of the god-things by whom I and all my corpse-kin were designed.

The stars shine high above my Rach Na'Schuul as they have done for years, for like this ruin they are slaves to perpetuity. They call these pockets of eternity Arcadia—but idylls they are not, for what is peace when I sleep circled by the dead, my Listener brethren of yore?

I shan't abandon Rach Na'Schuul; I *can't* abandon Rach Na'Schuul for I am bound to ruin by a quietus the hands of time would surely gift me if I did.

I sit, now, in the courtyard of a spire-keep and do as I have done for years—

I Listen. To a prelude long and dark.

A herald to a symphony of broken dreams.

Act I

Desolate Vignettes

Hounds

Avaria Norrith was dead. Or dreaming. For how else could he have come here to this meadow with its silver trees and ocean-colored grass? He looked down at Geph, his faithful longhound companion, and the gray-furred creature simply shrugged.

"Have you considered that you might be stoned beyond all comprehension?" Geph inquired. He did that a lot. Talking. Most longhounds retained some manner of silence even after they had learned to speak but Geph was the chatty exception. "Avaria?"

"You know I don't partake," Avaria said, starting slowly through the grass.

"Then why the hell am I talking?" the longhound asked.

"It's what you do."

"Well, if *you're* dead," Geph said, "then why am I here? Am I dead too?"

"Maybe?"

The longhound heaved a sigh that fell into a yawn. "Fuck it all, Avaria, what have you gotten us into this time?"

Avaria glared at him.

"I'm just saying."

"If you're talking about the time we were interned for defacing Virtuoso Khora's effigy," Avaria said, "let me please remind you it was *you* who climbed atop and took a massive, runny—"

"I was *drunk*," the longhound grumbled. "And the statue called my mother a bitch. What would you have done?"

Avaria rolled his eyes. "The effigies are incapable of speech, Geph. And your mother is a bitch. It's the proper term for a female hound."

"You keep saying that," Geph said, "and every time I believe you less."

Avaria shrugged. "Not my concern."

"It should be." Geph let out a hacking cough. "Where do you suppose we are?"

"If I were to venture a guess? The In Between," Avaria said.

"Then where hell is Equilibrium? I have a question."

"I can guarantee you, Geph, that Equilibrium remains incapable of manifesting you a jar of peanut butter," said Avaria, drawing a whine from the longhound. "Though I'm sure he'll oblige you with an ear scratch."

Geph gave a toothy grin.

They walked.

"It all feels the same," said Geph. "Have we actually gotten anywhere?"

"Not yet," said Avaria. He had come to this place enough to know the straightforward path was never as apparent as it seemed. "But we will."

You won't.

Avaria started at the words.

Geph cocked an eyebrow. "Are you okay?"

"You didn't hear that?" Avaria asked.

Geph tilted his head. "Because I'm a hound I'm supposed to have spectacular hearing, is that it? Well—"

How long have you been on this path, Avaria? How many years now? Days, weeks, and months spent trying to win the affections of a woman who could give two shits about you, hmm? And she had the gall to call herself your mother!

Avaria whirled around but there was no one there.

17

Search, but you'll not find me in the grass, hissed the voice. *I'm where I've always been — here, inside your head. Comfy, cozy in this prison that you've built. No — that* your mother *built. If she had loved you, where would you be now?*

Avaria shrieked. The meadow fell to ash, and from its ruin rose a silhouette of smoke and flame.

"I told you all those years ago," the figure said, *"that she would set me free."* It beckoned with an upturned palm and Geph obeyed, each step leaving gossamer threads of smoke. *"Faithful as always."*

Geph grinned at Avaria, green eyes glowing white, teeth like needles dripping blood.

Avaria retreated several steps. The figure and the hound advanced.

"You'll not escape, Avaria," the figure said.

Avaria turned—

"For I am legion here inside your head."

—sputtered, looking at the blade protruding from his chest.

"And there is nowhere you can hide that I can't find."

Crying now. He tasted blood and tears.

"For then what kind of vulture would I be?"

Darkness.

IT WAS COLD this night as Avaria walked the streets of Helveden, Geph beside him as he always was. His brow was slick with sweat, and his head stung something fierce. He'd had the dream again, stoked by vultures of his own design. Woken up retching in his chamber at the Hall, Geph whining on the other side of the door.

"Was it Wrath or Envy in the grass this time?" inquired Geph.

"An amalgamation of the two," Avaria said, fingering his chest. It was tender to the touch; he winced.

"Theories?"

"An answer," said Avaria. "The Virtuosos passed on me again the other night."

Geph nudged Avaria with his nose.

"Honestly... why'd she put me here if I'm never going to leave?"

"Your mother wants what's best for you, Avaria," said Geph.

"She's got a strange way of showing it," Avaria snapped. "Shoving me off to apprentice while Avaness and Maryn took

19

up arms and went to war for Ariath. I've been here half my life, a slave to erudition and abused by my own mind while they found glory in the heat of war. While *they* made mother proud."

"And you think swinging arms is all that draws your mother's praise?" Geph asked. "You think to her that mastering a blade is the be-all and end-all to life?"

Avaria scoffed. "In Ariath? Yes."

"I think you focus too much on the glory of war," said Geph. "Look around, Avaria. War destroys physically and mentally. Helveden stands half-erect, awaiting its resurrection by the Lightweavers who have drunk themselves into uselessness. The thought of facing vultures breeds fear, and that fear instills the urge to drink. It festers even now, an indomitable infection that has all but smothered Helveden's glow. Is that what you really want of yourself? To go off and come back like...that?"

"If it would make her proud..."

Geph sighed. "Oh, Avaria..."

They walked the rest of the way to the Bastion in silence, Geph stopping to sniff the occasional tree and Avaria brooding all the while. He fingered the summons in his coat pocket as they crossed a tree-lined courtyard wrought of white and scarlet stones arrayed in varying designs. What could the queen possibly need of him this late?

A frowning stewardess awaited their arrival. "You're an hour late."

Avaria shrugged. "I got lost along the way."

Geph nudged him firmly in the leg with his nose.

"Fine," Avaria sighed. "I was drunk in bed and dreaming of the end."

The stewardess curled her upper lip and rolled her eyes. "Follow me."

She led them through the Bastion, glorious in its whites and reds and various depictions of the raven god to whom they all implored. It was paradise where the Hall of Light-weavers was eternal hell.

Further and further, they went. The walls, ceiling, and floor fell to a deep red. Avaria had never been to this part of the Bastion before, which was saying a lot. As a child he'd wandered where his legs and the Bastion staff would allow.

They came to a circular stark white door inlaid with glyphs and grooves. The stewardess extended a glowing index finger and traced the innermost glyph. Illumination swam through the grooves and into the outlying glyphs. The door dilated, revealing the chamber beyond. The stewardess dragged him inside. Geph stayed put.

Avaria eyed three women sitting at the far end of the room. *Shit.*

"Ah. We were wondering if and when you might arrive," said Virtuoso Khal.

"I was not so confident as Virtuoso Khal and Queen Ahnil," said Norema Sel, the shortest of the three. She dismissed the stewardess with a nod, leaving Avaria to the wolves.

Wolf, really.

He eyed the queen. "Hello, mother."

AVARIA STARED AT the queen. He hadn't seen her in at least a half-dozen years. She looked older in the eyes though no less hawkish and intimidating. Reluctantly, if not slightly mockingly, he touched his right hand to his left shoulder in the formal salute.

"How may I be of service?"

Norema Sel gestured to an open chair at the table. "Sit."

Avaria gave her a prolonged stare before accommodating her request. He hadn't seen *her* in a while either. His heart fluttered momentarily. They'd been a pair at one time. A secret kept in shadows, for what would people think if they knew General Sel had shared her bed with *him,* the Norrith family castoff?

"Virtuoso Khal says you're developing well," Norema said.

"*Have developed,*" his mother said. "You're able to wield mirkúr as I understand it."

"Have been for ages," Avaria said, picking at a loose fingernail.

The queen drew her lips to a thin line.

"You say that with such nonchalance, Avaria, that it suggests ignorance on your part," Norema said. "There are very few left who can do what you do, let alone as an apprentice."

Avaria considered her words. "It isn't ignorance Nor— *General.* I'm simply indifferent. What does it matter if I'm able to wield The Raven's Wings? Mastering illum and mirkúr has gotten me nowhere. I'm almost thirty years of age and the Hall sees fit to keep me there until I die."

An exaggeration, but it often felt like he would never leave.

Virtuoso Khal offered a sympathetic nod. "Apprenticeships at the Hall are notoriously demanding, but they can ill afford to be otherwise." She passed him a slip of parchment. "We have need of you, Avaria."

"It's time for you to spread your wings, so to speak," Norema said.

Avaria scanned the parchment. His eyes went wide.

"A simple yes will do," his mother said.

Avaria looked at the women. "I—"

"Unless you aren't up to it," Norema said. There was a glint in her red eyes.

Avaria slipped the parchment into his pocket. "Of course, I am."

"Excellent." Norema gestured toward the door. "We'll be in touch."

Avaria stood and gave the formal salute. Then he withdrew.

"You haven't said a word since we left the Bastion," Geph said.

Avaria nodded. He was prone to withdrawing into himself in times of stress.

"Avaria?" Geph poked him in the leg with his nose. "What is it?"

"Have you heard of The Raven's Rage?" Avaria asked.

"In passing," Geph said. "What of it?"

"They, um..." Avaria swallowed. "They want me to forge it."

Geph gaped. "A weapon? *That* weapon? Why?"

"I don't know."

"Are you going to?" Geph asked.

A light snow fell, dusting Avaria's hair and shoulders as he walked. "Maybe."

Geph whined. "You already told them you would. I know you did, Avaria. I can smell the truth on you a mile away." He snapped at a snowflake. "It's personal, isn't it? Of course it is. Avaria, your mother—"

"She needs to see!" Avaria snapped. "I need her to see in me what she saw in Avaness and Maryn. I want to do something she'll be proud of, Geph. I just..." Avaria heaved a sigh into the frosty night. "I want her to want me like she did them."

Geph licked Avaria's hand.

"You head on back to the Hall," Avaria said. "I need some time to think."

* * *

AVARIA HAD ALWAYS found solace in the woods, in the trees beneath the sway of night. Unlike Helveden they enfolded him in silence and allowed him peace enough to think. To brood as he was wont to do. To waltz with the monsters of his mind as they made manifest at his side.

"Envy, Pride, and Wrath," Avaria greeted. They followed him as hounds, threads of mirkúr trailing their wake. He made no move to banish them but held his arms out wide. "What do you think? Should I oblige them, forge this weapon they so *desperately* desire?"

Wrath snarled.

"It *would* make them see," Avaria agreed.

Pride snapped its teeth.

"True. I *am* the utmost of apprentices."

Envy whined.

"Swallow your fear," Avaria hissed. If he were to fail... "I need to be worthy. She needs to see me as more than just a thing she found in the woods. If I were to perish, would she care? Would—"

Pride growled. Wrath and Envy bared their teeth-like-knives as a distant-growing-nearer shriek destroyed the forest calm. Avaria formed a thread of mirkúr to a blade; he advanced behind the hounds.

At length the trees fell to ruin, and they entered a glade. At the center stood a shrine; before the shrine there knelt a girl. Avaria and the hounds approached with heed. His mirkúr pulsed with every step; the hounds dripped ichor from their mouths.

"Who are you?" Avaria asked.

The girl turned. Her eyes were dead moons, and her flesh was burnt paper; her hair hung in silver strands. She cocked her head.

Avaria held his blade between them. "I asked—"

"We in this moment depart," the girl rasped, "replacing all that we are."

She stood and took a step toward Avaria, dark energy enfolding her from head to toe. Where once her face had been now hung a snow-white shroud; and from her back, six wings of black.

The hounds dissolved in her presence.

Avaria fell to his knees beneath her sway, cold in his bones. What was she?

"Are you going to kill me?"

She approached and pulled him up into a cold embrace,

whispering, "Listen to your dreams, for things are never as they seem. We in this moment depart, replacing all that we are...."

She was gone, and Avaria was holding mist.

She

The meadow.

Avaria was alone save a bird in a tree. A raven. It blinked its beady eyes and squawked.

"Am I supposed to understand any of that?" Avaria asked.

The raven clucked. It abandoned its perch in favor of Avaria's shoulder, digging its talons into his flesh. Avaria cursed and the bird snapped its beak. He shooed the stupid thing but that only served to tighten its grip. Avaria hissed.

"Ease up, all right? What do you want of me?"

The raven gestured with its wing.

"A tree," Avaria said. "What about it?"

More talons. An authoritative squawk.

"Okay, okay!" Avaria approached the tree in all its silver majesty. He felt a sense of peace beneath its branches. Peace, with undertones of... something. He couldn't quite put his finger on it.

The raven offered a soft cluck.

"Did something happen here?" Avaria asked.

"More than you know," the raven said, and Avaria jumped. *"Compose yourself."*

Avaria massaged the spot between his eyes. Talking birds. Had he gotten drunk before bed again?

"We in this moment depart," the raven said, *"replacing all that we are. It would do you well to remember that. Lest she leads you through a forest dark."*

"Lest who?" Avaria asked. "The girl from the woods? That... *thing*?"

"Stay vigilant, Avaria Norrith, for things aren't always what they seem."

The raven gave a great flap, ascending as The In Between was cloaked in flames.

MIDMORNING.

Avaria sipped of his flask. He'd gotten fuck-all for sleep; had sat awake in bed pondering the girl-thing in the woods and the raven in his dream—his *new* dream. Word for word, they had said the exact same thing.

"We in this moment depart...replacing all that we are."

"Cryptic," offered Geph as they strolled the western grounds. The Hall was the city's pride and joy, though its occupants were often devoid of both. Fifty weeks of intellectual abuse quelled even the strongest of wills.

"Hmm."

"Are you *sure* you weren't—"

"Stoned beyond belief? No, Geph, I'm *quite sure* I wasn't."

Geph yawned. "What do you think it—er, *she* was? Demon of some sort?"

"Doubt it," Avaria said. "Haven't seen vultures in these parts for years."

War and extinction had a very intimate relationship.

"Spirit?" Geph asked.

"Maybe." Avaria stroked his chin. "Though it's been at least a dozen years since I encountered one, and it looked nothing like the girl I saw last night. And the way she..." He trailed off. He'd neglected telling Geph about his hounds.

The longhound cocked an eyebrow.

Avaria sighed. "The way she dispersed my hounds with her sheer presence"—Geph barked objectionably—"put fear in me like I've never felt before. Have you ever been cold in your bones?"

"I can't say that I have," said Geph, "but more important-ly—"

"I was a mix of things last night," Avaria said. "I didn't mean to let them come—"

"But you made no try to hold them back," said Geph. "I know you better than you know yourself sometimes, Avaria. I'm one-hundred and fifty years old—I can *literally* smell bull-shit a mile away."

"Does it help if I tell you they were leashed?"

Geph narrowed his eyes. "How the fuck does one *leash* a sinhound?"

Avaria tapped his head. "In all the time you've known me, Geph, have I ever—*ever*—let them run amok? Have I ever hurt anyone beneath their sway?"

"No," the longhound muttered. "But you *have* let them in-fluence the way you live your life. Holding onto all that rage, all that pent up frustration and jealousy—you're only making them stronger, Avaria, and that's the part that frightens me the most. One day you'll lose control, and the hounds will sow slaughter unlike anything you've seen before."

"And how—"

"I've fucking *seen* unbounded sinhounds in my time. *Long*

before I came to be your friend. *Long before* your mother came to be." Geph sighed, a faraway look manifesting in his eyes. "She was a good girl. But she couldn't quell them in the end."

"Geph—"

"I've a thing or two to take care of," Geph said, breaking from Avaria.

Avaria stopped and watched the longhound trot the opposite direction.

Rain fell.

It was going to be a long day.

"I'LL DO IT," said Avaria. "On the condition that you tell me what it's for."

"Temporal alteration," said Norema. "The chance to rewrite history and prevent the vultures' wrath." She leaned across the table so their noses nearly touched. "To bring back those we've lost."

Avaria blinked. He hadn't expected such a forthcoming, if not ludicrous response. "Is... is that even possible?"

"Anything is possible," said Virtuoso Khal, "when one possesses possibility itself."

Maybe *they* were stoned.

"The Raven's Rage is more than just a weapon," said the queen. "It is a key."

"*The* key," Norema said.

Avaria paused for a breath. "How does it work? How do you intend to rewrite time?"

"With enough energy it will open a way to the Temporal Sea," said Virtuoso Khal. "And through the Sea we'll sail to where it all went wrong, and the darkness roused from sleep. We'll slay the beast before it wakes."

Now they *really* sounded stoned—but Avaria was intrigued. *Avaness. Maryn.* Could he bring them back? So many years alone. So many years reliving the news of their demise. Confined to the darkness of the Hall. Not even his mother had come.

"*Your life could be different,*" said Wrath.

"*You could be with your blood,*" Envy hissed.

"*You could be* free," suggested Pride.

Free. Of these chains. Of this loneliness. Of this loveless life to which he'd been condemned. Better to have to died in the snow that fateful night than to have wound up here.

"I'll do it," Avaria reaffirmed. "Just point me on my way."

AVARIA WALKED THE Bastion courtyard at a measured pace, burdened with purpose for the first time in his life. In the depths and darkness of the Peaks of Dren, he would find the fragments of that old and ill-used sword, and with them forge a life worth living.

"Even when your steps are slow, you're faster than most."

Avaria turned to the voice, waited as the queen approached.

"Quick when silent," said Avaria. "Lest the Virtuosos beat you."

His mother winced.

"You seem surprised," Avaria said. "Or is that guilt?"

She said nothing. Avaria walked and she attended him.

"What we ask of you... it will be arduous."

"I know," Avaria said. "And I can handle it. I've trained and studied far too long to fail. But you only know that secondhand. Because you ordered Virtuoso Khal to keep you up to speed. Do I embarrass you? Does it make you ill to pay me mind? It seems to me we only speak when it's convenient."

The queen frowned. "You know you don't, Avaria. You could never—"

"Then why the distance all these years?" Avaria hissed.

"Fifteen years, mother. Fifteen years of torment in the form of erudition while Avaness and Maryn reaped glory and affection here at home!"

Avaria yelped; his cheek stung. His mother held her left hand firm and ready for another go. "How dare you... How dare you speak ill of the dead. Of your broth—"

"You struck me..." The words felt strange as they left his tongue. In all his years she had never hit him once. He touched his cheek and turned away, left his mother standing in the courtyard as the shock withered and the pain bloomed.

Walked.

Walked until he reached the Hall.

Until he reached his favorite tree at the northmost end of the grounds.

He cried.

AN OLD CITY.

A grand city.

A *dead* city.

Avaria blinked. He was dreaming, but he had never dreamt this place before. A necropolis beneath a sky that threatened rain, the skeletons of spires rising as if the ruin were the maw of something monstrous. Instinct drew him inward, and he walked with measured steps, the stillness sending shivers up his spine.

At the center of the city stood the greatest spire of them all. Despite the ruination it was mostly intact. Avaria touched the wall; whispers kissed his ears, and a feeling of dread entombed his heart. There was sorrow here inside the stones; fear and fury warred for rule.

"This place was beautiful once."

Avaria turned to the voice and met a man with midnight-feathered wings. There was a gentle melancholy to his face; his eyes were two gray pools of woe.

"They call me Ruin King. They call me Alerésh the Dread." He held his arms out wide. "I have done horrible things."

Avaria frowned. "I—"

"What do you mean?" a second softer voice inquired. "Why are we here?"

Avaria started as a figure passed through him; he realized he was little more than a ghost.

"We were rotten, she and I." Alerésh closed his eyes. "We envisioned life, yet from our hubris we birthed only ash. Ash—and annihilation like this world has never known." He opened his eyes. "He quelled the malediction once, but you will not do so again. The hounds hunger—and they are near.

"*She* is near."

SCREAM.

Like an infant kissed by flames.

Scream.

Scream.

SCREAM.

SHE LEFT HIM by the tree beneath which he slept.

Her wings trailed behind her like the train of a tattered gown.

"So much ruin." Her voice was ash in the wind; it ached to speak.

She walked—through the darkness, kissed by shadows she had mothered for millennia.

She dwelled—in thoughts of geneses and ends, of hounds and fowl.

She died—

and was reborn.

No sleep.

Anathema

One life lost this night. One friend.

Erath spat into the snow, jaw quivering. Tears streaked her cheeks. How could this have happened? How could a simple walk have ended like... like *this*? Sinhounds. Fucking sinhounds. Fucking *demons*. There hadn't been demons in the Peaks of Dren for decades. So why now, of all days? Leru's birthday—the queen's *youngest daughter's* birthday. She grabbed a fistful of snow and hurled it into the night.

Footsteps.

Erath glanced at the source, sighing. "Serenae."

She regarded Erath with eyes the color of moonlit snow. Had they been darker, she and Erath might very well have been twins. They had always been of similar guise.

"They're going to light the pyres soon," said Serenae.

Erath closed her eyes. "What must Queen Silith think of

me..."

Serenae wrapped her arms around Erath. "Nothing so ill as you might concoct. You were ambushed, Erath. You were preyed upon by nightmares come to life. How could you— how could *anyone* have foreseen such a monstrous thing?"

"Illumancy?" said Erath.

"You know that isn't how it works," Serenae said. "Not anymore..."

"I know," Erath whispered. "But... demons. After all this time."

"There *is* something wrong—of that I have no doubt." Serenae pulled Erath to her feet. "But for the moment it can wait. We need to say goodbye."

Goodbye. Such a horribly finite word. In this moment Erath loathed it as the sunlight loathed her flesh. She trailed Serenae with sullen steps. She sensed tonight was just the beginning.

ERATH HATED SONGS for the simple fact the only songs her people sung were requiems and the last two songs she'd heard were requiems for friends.

Fire danced; shadows waltzed. They consumed Leru, devoured flesh made dead by demons so her spirit could ascend. *Ascend to what?* Erath watched, hands clasped behind her back, as drenarian throngs paid reverence to Leru. Tears. Prayers. Recollections of a fabricated friendship and a countless many men proclaiming their undying love. *Fucking idiots. Fucking frauds.* A show to curry favor with the king and queen.

She sought them out beside the blaze. Fenrin, silver-eyed and wolfish in the face. Silith, yellow-eyed and hawkish. It made sense considering the bestial shapes they took. They regarded her with solemn stares; Erath bowed her head in reverent guilt. She continued to the altar, spellbound by the azure flames in which the princess burned.

"Why did she have to die?" Erath started at the inquiry, at Silith's hand upon her own. "My youngest, Erath—why?" Erath sensed no accusation in her tone, yet still she felt the phantom strings of culpability tugging on her soul.

"...My fault," she whispered to the queen. To no one. To the night.

"Erath..."

"There were so many... and I couldn't—"

She pulled away from the queen. Ran from the flames. Through snow and darkness like the coward that she was.

THE WISPLANDS LAY southeast of Nil-Illúm. They were a haven, a remnant of her life before the Burn. Cloaked in wisplight, they were sheltered from the sun; *she* was sheltered from the sun.

Erath strolled through wisplit snow, enfolded in a black cloak the queen's eldest daughter, Alor, had gifted to her some years back; Alor was dead. Erath wore the garment when the weight of life seemed its heaviest.

At length she came to a henge of midnight-colored stones. Three total, each depicting a figure cloaked and winged. They had been a source of intrigue for years; encircled in their primordial majesty she felt a sense of peace unique unto the Wisplands and the henge. She sat now in the snow, legs crossed, hands resting on her knees. Body trembling, breathing soft. Eyes closed and swathed in the darkness of her mind.

Think, she urged, *of something bright. Soft and bright like illum on a summer night. Like wisplight in the darkness of the trees.* Like Alor holding baby Leru. Like Leru holding a fox in the days before the Burn. Like the days before the Burn.

Blood on her tongue. Erath cursed and opened her eyes. Spat red in the snow. "Why?" she hissed. "How?" That was the utmost of questions, the ghost of yesteryears that trailed her like a hungry dog. How had a sword managed the Burn? She gnashed her teeth at the memory of a nameless man, the wielder of The Raven's Rage. Long dead, buried in the ashes of his folly, yet anathema to Erath even now.

"Erath."

She started at her name. Turned to see a young woman. Eyes like fire, black of hair. Pale—paler than Erath who was paler than snow. Pack on her shoulder, blade on her waist.

"Rowe." She approached her friend.

"Been a while," said Rowe. "Little less than seven years. How've you been?"

Erath cackled. Clapped a hand to her mouth. Eyes narrowed; vision obstructed by tears. Weakness. Disgusted by the cracks. What a fragile, ugly thing. What an ugly thing fragility was...

"Erath..." Rowe took her hand.

"Leru is dead," said Erath. "And..." Nothing—and nothing. What else was there?

Rowe pulled her into a tight embrace; Erath melted. "I'm so sorry."

"...Feels like things are..." Were what? "It feels like all

those years ago." The lead-up to the Burn. Madness, monsters. "Why are they back, Rowe? Sinhounds. Why the *fuck* are they back—and why did they have to take Leru?" She pulled away from Rowe. "Why are *you* back?"

"Questions," Rowe said. "Questions that need answering." She pulled her collar down to reveal black mottling encircling her neck. "It should have faded, but it's the angriest it's been."

The words chilled Erath. It was the mark of Te Mirkvahíl. She brushed the blighted skin; Rowe winced but made no move to push her hand away. "You killed Te Mirkvahíl."

"Did I?" Rowe took a seat in the snow; Erath joined her. "I've been having nightmares. Dreams that feel like something more. Like..." She shook her head. "Like what I see has happened once before, one way or another. I can feel it in my bones."

"And what do you dream?" Erath asked.

"Of hounds and fowl and a sword that shouldn't be."

A memory of light; a memory of pain. "The Raven's Rage."

Rowe looked her in the eyes. "It's somewhere in the Peaks. Every nightmare leads me closer, Erath. It whispers in my sleep. It..." She looked away. "You must think I'm mad."

Erath took her hand. "Never."

Silence. Wisplit solace. It was easier to breathe.

"Rowe?"

"Hmm?"

"I missed you."

Squeeze of the hand.

Dancing wisps and memories of sunsets in the fall.

"Will you come with me, Erath?"

To chase a whispering dream? To find the blade anathema?

"Yes." Erath wanted answers—and she wanted them in blood.

SCREAMS—AVELINE HEARD THEM even now, millennia removed.

Ash—she felt it even now, their remnants tickling her face.

How many years? How many centuries more of suffering would she endure? She cared little for this wasteland she had wrought; little for the people she had met and even less for the people she had killed. This reality was a flaw, and yet—she wrestled. With herself. With the voices in her head. With her hounds and fowl of smoke. She wrestled, and her skull ached every moment of the day, every moment of the night. Ached with the coldness of regret, with the fire of intent.

With the numbness borne of weariness, uncertainty, and grief.

"I will save you," she uttered to dead people from dead days, and her words were children looking on the corpses of their kin—wishful but unsure.

"Rowe?"

She looked at the girl called Erath; for a moment, felt the misery in her stare. Knives of sorrow biting through her flesh at the loss of sweet Leru. For once, a death *not* on Aveline's conscience. What, then, had slain the girl?

Again, Erath beckoned to her guise. "Not much further—come."

Aveline smiled wearily and walked.

The sky hemorrhaged. Beads of crimson kissed her face—softly, as Alor had long ago. Before the Burn. Before the soldiers gut her in the snow and left her in the sunlight for the carrion birds and flies.

Still, Aveline walked.

Still, history screamed.

Hush

Gil'an Mor, City of Hounds, was dead. Had been for millennia, since before the time of Dren. High-walled, guarded by statues of Ybot, Mother of Hounds, Reader of Time, First of Her Kind.

Mother of Geph.

"You called me here," he whispered to the ruin, to the memories roiling in his head. "I forsook my friend to walk your streets, to see what secrets you still keep. Please—come to me. Lead me on my way." The hush of Gil'an Mor endured; Geph shivered. "So be it."

He would go it alone.

AZURE STREETS INFECTED with geodes. Windows void of light.

A million Threads adrift, like corpses in the sea. Dead and bloated with the history of Gil'an Mor. Ghosts of longhounds past. Geph whimpered at their touch, for every kiss invoked

47

its master's doom, put voice to something old. Words like wind-churned ash and gutted crows.

"You..." he whispered to the hush of Gil'an Mor. "Are you here?"

Threads of memory licked his ears—the Quietus of All. Crystal corpses crumbling in Her wake. Her She It—The Demoness of Down Below; The Beast of Underlight; this *thing* that they had leashed 'neath moons of yore.

A hand of Threads to lead him on. A curling finger beckoned. Geph obliged.

To the Angelarium he went.

A HALL OF effigies, tall and dead. Hounds of feathered wings and halos wrought from stars. So much time had Geph spent here, wishing he were of their ilk. That he could sail the skies as Ybot, Ykoms, and Ymmas had done. He was Geph, son of Ybot—but of her majesty, his blood was filled with none. He had been the weakest of them all, and yet—he and he alone remained.

"We were great once," Geph said. "The future. Greater than the Reshapers, even. We could have changed the world— literally. But with you went the science of revision; we cannot rewrite our ills."

And that was why this business with The Raven's Rage disturbed him so. How did they expect to *literally* rewrite time with *that*—this blade of old which, last time used, had seen the drenarians devoured by the sun?

'Thus the Peaks of Dren do dwell in night etern,' recited Geph. Many a tragedy chronicled the drenarians' cruel demise—were they players in this new game too? Geph urged his dreams to show him something more. Threads of distant memories, condemned to Underlight millennia ago, acknowledged him with whispers in the tongue of Mor:

"Descend and see—seek relics 'neath expired light, O Child of Ybot."

Through ruined halls they went, every pawstep arousing pastel echoes of the past. They regarded Geph and his Threadwrought guide with idle stares, uniform in quietus; faded back to whence they'd come. He longed to free them from this place; he longed to free Gil'an Mor of itself—but such a thing was difficult and required answers from below.

They descended.

Memories screamed.

* * *

THEY WHISPER OF me.

They whisper and they stare.

Things. Hound-things. Graceful beasts beguiled by the ills of all.

Kismet. This place called Gil'an Mor—this realm of Underlight. That I should rouse here 'mongst these lesser things, these hounds of sin. That I should rouse here after burning for millennia in tortured sleep.

Kismet, that I should catch her

staring through

the dark.

Staring.

Burning.

Gods, I'm burning.

She is ash.

Gone.

Memory.

Dead. Just...

Dead.

Kismet.

LET.

ME.

OUT.

SCREAMS.

They burn.

SCREAMS.

They cower.

Cower like the beasts, the noble hounds they are.

Mine.

HUSH.

Kismet. Dead place. Dead place full of hush.

Hush

Hush.

HUSH.

An epithet.

I am Hush.

Free.

GEPH FLED THE corpse of Gil'an Mor. Crashed through trees. Smacked streams. Itched—itched like hell. Sin crawling in his flesh—the touch of that *thing*. His leash. Tripped, rolled.

Swathed in mud. Smelled the rot of yore, escaping memories of Gil'an Mor, strong like sunbaked corpses cloaked in shit.

Voice like fly-kissed salted honey in his ears.

Yelped, howled, whimpered like the pup he hadn't been for years. Mother—mama, mama, mama. Nothing else and no one else he wanted more. To hold him, clean his fur and tell him all was well and right.

Voice like dying in his ears. Crooning of a carrion thing.

Geph pushed himself to stand. To see this nightmare that had come, this thing that'd found him in the dead and dark and sorrow of the woods surrounding Gil'an Mor. Eyes like coins alight and feathered wings that fell to smoke. Tattered flesh of flame and Thread, of time and stars.

Voice like virgin snowfall in the dead of winter night in his ears.

"Quietus," whispered Geph.

"Hush."

She beckoned.

He obliged. She reeked of memory, stoked his gluttony, his need to feed—to drink of yesteryears and feel the brilliant warmth of Gil'an Mor as once she'd stood.

To see his mother. Hear her. Kiss her.

Voice like feathers, leaves enraptured by a breeze in his ears.

They went.

Cacophony

Snow.

Silence.

Avaria departed Helveden draped in both. He walked alone; Geph had business elsewhere. So be it. Avaria was used to solitude—it ruled his life. He pulled his cloak tighter. Retreated further into the dark of his hood and breathed. Tension dripped away like rivulets of sweat; purpose bloomed—find the sword. Find the fragments with which freedom would be forged.

He gazed south through darkness fleeting at the touch of infant dawn. South toward peaks of ruin in which ruined people dwelled. The drenarians—he could fix them if he tried. If he wrought The Raven's Rage, he could slaughter misery and mend mistakes. Find freedom in a world renewed. Genesis in restoration.

If there was any truth. Who but the gods could rewrite history—and even then, to what extent? Here they were—here *he* was seeking fragments of a madman's folly for a gambit predicated on a hope. A desperate dream the ink of yore could be erased, replaced with something better than before.

He walked.

Clouds hemorrhaged.

Still, he walked.

NIGHT LIKE THE snow-choked abyss.

A road of blood and screaming trees.

The trek to Ulm had been a joyless blur of his design. Misery was motivation. Avaria clung to dreams of ruin like a leech to flesh. Lingered on the sting of his mother's hand across his face. He'd thought of nothing else for the past two days; he'd slept for less than half.

Ulm was dead; had been since the war. A dead place filled with dead things. A sepulcher abandoned to the hands of time, as was much of Ariath in the wake of bladed dread. He trekked with idle hands; the sinhounds roused inside his mind. Hissed. Snarled. Unintelligible yet persuasive all the same. They came like smoke. Whimpered at the stench of dead Ulm. Disappeared.

What, Avaria asked them, *do you fear?*

"*Mother Sin,*" said Wrath.

"*Leave Ulm lest she leash us to her will,*" begged Pride.

"*Lest she leash* you, *Avaria,*" said Envy.

A cacophony of fear. His skull ached.

He left. East. North.

A tree in the shadow of the Peaks. Gnarled and twisted like the tentacle of something old. Eldritch whispers tickling memories awake; soothing him to sleep. He sheltered in its oaken void, enfolded in the dark and silence of his cloak. Slept. Dreamt. Awoke.

Walked.

Dawn wept silent snow.

Still, he walked.

Turn, the daylight whispered.

Turn, his instincts hissed.

So, he did.

The sinhounds shrieked.

Still, he walked

Ulm called.

IN THE DEAD and dark he found her corpse—that girl of burnt

paper flesh. In the dead and dark of Ulm she did remain, ravaged by the claws of something bestial and mad. Avaria walked to the center of the necropolis, sinhounds screaming all the while. What had brought him here? What had turned him from his path?

He trekked through weathered gore and rock, through streets of ash and bone, old mirkúr slick and thick like rain-borne mud. The rib-cage remnants of the church appeared, a sullen beacon in the wake of war. The jagged ruin called to him; the sinhounds howled; his skull ached.

Still, he walked.

Once, as a boy, he had come to Ulm. And once, as a boy, the city had been beautiful—a stone-wrought tapestry of reds and whites where dead kings slept, and warriors were born. Dawnbringers, Aegises, and in between.

"You called me here," he said. "Why?"

Whispers slithered from the church; kissed his ears like sirens.

Avaria held his ground. "Come to me. Whatever you are, come to me."

Whimpering. Sorrow. Trapped inside—the way was shut.

Avaria tensed his jaw, formed a mirkúr blade. Curiosity

pushed him toward the church. Inside. Further yet, within the bowels of ruined sanctification. Inlays, effigies—laid waste by war and time.

He came to a chamber guarded by a door inlaid with wards—dying glyphs that thirsted for his light. He pressed his palm to the door; illum streamed from his fingertips, filling the patterned grooves. The door groaned, dilated to reveal a room—and a floating head, preserved in twisting energy the color of a cloudless midday sky.

Avaria arched his brow. He entered at a measured pace, arm and blade extended fully. Whispers. Shards of shadowed recollections emanating from the head. Avaria winced at the onslaught, staggered. Pressed himself against the wall to keep from falling.

Bright eyes. Like the roiling sea beneath the sun, a swirl of greens and grays and blues. Bright, but weary. They regarded him with... what? Curiosity? Ragged desperation? Either way, Avaria felt compelled to push the crashing memories back and pluck the head from rest. It called to him in a way he could not yet define. He steeled himself and grasped it by its gnarled and braided hair.

It gasped; Avaria yelped, nearly dropped the fucking

thing. Garbled language trickled from its mouth; threads of pale blue luminesence clung to strands of hair. Its eyes rolled independent of the other.

Avaria grimaced, held it level with his own. "What... who—"

"*Ssswwwooorrrd...*" Panting. Gasping. "*SsssswooOrd.*"

Avaria narrowed his eyes. "Do you mean The Raven's Rage—*that* sword?"

Rictus, wheezing like the dead—the maybe sort of who-the-fuck-knew what. "*Fffiiinnnd... ssswwwooorrrddd... Ss-saaave...*"

Silence. Sleeping—dead? Avaria sighed, tucked the head away inside his pack.

The sinhounds wailed yet.

He retreated from the church. Past her corpse—that girl of burnt paper flesh. Fled the dark and dead of Ulm, half-relieved, half-disappointed to have not encountered Mother Sin, this thing his hounds so passionately feared.

It snowed—and he walked.

Still, he walked.

Melancholia

I found myself by losing hope."

Erath could not remember where she had read that, but it stuck with her as she and Rowe traversed the Wisplands. Enfolded in the cloak Alor had gifted her some years ago, never had she felt more lost.

"Was this what the Peaks were like?" Rowe asked. "Before the Burn?"

Sunshine just beyond the wisplight ward. Erath took a deep breath, exhaled slowly through her teeth. "Yes. The Wisplands are a remnant of better days."

"Is there no way to harness the wisplight?"

Erath smiled sadly. "If there is, we've yet to find it." She looked at Rowe. "You dreamt again last night."

Rowe nodded. Ring-eyed, red-eyed, sunken like a ghoul. Looked as though she'd aged a year or two in sleep. "An isle in the clouds. A dead city."

"How does that relate to the sword?" Erath asked. "You said it was here in the Peaks."

Rowe shrugged. "Could be that the isle is above the Peaks. I'm not sure; I only know of what I dreamt—and what I dreamt begs that I ascend. That *we* ascend."

Silence.

They walked; wisplight danced.

"It all goes downhill so fast, doesn't it?" Erath asked. "One day everything is all and well and the next it's just... not. And the ills of the world begin to bleed into one another and soon enough it's hard to remember the moments of peace because the darkness is so overwhelmingly profound."

She flashed pale skin. "I haven't seen the world in years, Rowe—*truly* seen it. How could I when the Burn confined me to a rock? Too long beneath the sun and my fate is the same as Alor's—just... ash."

"The world is an unkind place full of unkind people and unkind things." There was a bitterness to Rowe's words, as unfamiliar as it was intense. She flexed her jaw. "I saw things while I was gone. Things that made me wonder whether revising history would be the proper thing to do if it were possible. Rewrite everything—start from scratch..."

She looked at Erath and her eyes were wet. "I loved some-one. We had a child, and everything was nice, and the world was beautiful across the sea. And then..."

Erath stopped, pulled Rowe into a firm embrace; held her as she shook, and fresh snowfall kissed their hair and cheeks.

"The world is dying," Rowe whispered, "and I want to fix it. Right wrongs, put families back together, raise the dead who died before their time—*just fucking fix it all.*"

"Me too," Erath murmured. "Me too." Would that she could—*You would rewrite history?* she asked herself. *Just like that—without a second thought?*

Yes. The reply came with far more certainty than Erath had expected, but how else should she have answered? How else could she have responded to a question so direct?

"What do you think it means," she started, pulling away from Rowe, "to find oneself by losing hope?"

For as long as Erath had known her, Rowe had enjoyed philosophical inquiries and commentaries. Something sooth-ing about them.

"There are infinite interpretations," Rowe said, "but to me it means dwelling in darkness so profound we learn how in-tense our resolve is; we see our character at its most vulnerable and honest."

"To me as well," Erath said.

Rowe gave Erath's cheek a light caress. "We should keep on."

Erath nodded.

They walked.

AVELINE THIRSTED FOR The Raven's Rage in the way she longed to hold her husband, Beht, and her son Jor; to kiss Alor—desperately, enough so she would raze this world to see them, feel them, hear them.

She urged her dreams to lead her on, to point her toward this cloud-swathed, sky-bound isle she had seen. It was there—she could feel it in her borrowed bones. The means to reclamation.

She snuck a backward glance at Erath, the sweet young woman. She reeked of melancholia in a way that few could understand—but Aveline did, and she yearned to ease her pain for simple fact she bore Erath and her people no ill will. They had accepted her as one of their own those years before the Burn. Save Alor, it was *Erath* who had been her closest friend.

But she couldn't know what Aveline had become. She couldn't know what monster hopelessness had made her. What her monstrousness had made her do to Rowe.

She clutched a silver pendant around her neck—a gift of yore from Beht. *You would do the same, would you not?* She paused, as if waiting for the silence to reply. *I know you would. Please tell me you would...*

She heaved a sigh to the mountain wind and thought.

Dreamt.

Just...

Dreamt.

THEY COME. THEY seek this thing of misery and wrath, of possibility and hope. I am duty-sworn to keep it... yet I know not if I can. The songs of old, the symphonies of Rach Na'Schuul do not resound as once they did; the crystals have run dry—I am weak. Finite. The last of the Etheri kind.

I dream of snow and stars, of nights beside the lake.

I dream of Banerowos as she stood before the cull, before the gods went mad and killed us all.

I dream of Sonja, my beloved daughter murdered in the sorrow of the woods. Hung by the man to whom she gave her heart, from whom she gained a name.

I dream of worlds. Realities not my own, yet from mine they were born. From the Fountainhead they came, myriad conjurings of desperation, woe, and might. Might—for the mad ones who discern the means to rewrite time are mighty things indeed.

I dream here in this Pocket of Arcadia, this place beyond the rules of time. I dream here of the Fountainhead and the day it all went wrong—the day that wrought a million times a million realities and worlds.

I dream here and I know—

the cycle never ends.

Nameless

A cave somewhere in the Peaks.

Darkness save a single wisp of illum.

Two days up through rock and snow. In mountain-manufactured gloom. In silence and in pain. Rolled ankle, sprained neck—lucky it wasn't worse, that fall. Avaria leaned against the wall, weary but well-fed; fuck, but he'd had a lot of dried meat since leaving Helveden. Dried meat and water smelling mildly of maybe still ripe lemon. What luxury, this princely life he led...

He sat there, looking at the severed head his trek through Ulm had gifted him. Silent, dead-eyed, pale as death, leaking energy in threads—what was this thing? *Who* was this thing—this thing that clearly knew about the sword? Not a peep since then, since emerging from the dead and dark of Ulm—was that it, then? Avaria nudged it lightly with the toe of his boot.

"Going to say something? *Do* something?"

Cough. Ash-dust in the air. Avaria jumped. It regarded him with... what?

"...*uuuggg*..." it moaned. Cough. More ash-dust, motes of infant light; dull like dying eyes, but brilliant in the gloom. "...*UUUGGG*..." Hack-cough. Something like bile but... not. *"FUUUUCK."*

Avaria pressed against the wall. "Fuck is right!"

The head rose several feet, propelled by threads of light. Bright eyes, like the roiling sea beneath the sun. Hawkish in the face. It blew a loose strand of hair out of its eyes. "Who the fuck," it rasped, "are you?"

Avaria cocked an eyebrow, keen to draw a blade. "Who the fuck are *you*?"

"I..."—hack-cough, ash-dust—"asked you first?"

"I saved you," said Avaria. "Think that counts for something, hmm?"

Faraway look in those beautiful maelstrom eyes. "Saved me..." Soft voice. Puzzled. Disoriented—eyes betrayed as such. Horribly so. "Saved me from... what? Where?"

Avaria swallowed, took a deep breath. Eased his blood. "The church. Beneath Ulm. Not sure from what, if anything at all." A lie? Maybe. Maybe there'd been something there, this Mother Sin the hounds so passionately feared. "Where's the rest of you?"

Glazed eyes. "The rest of me..." Cough. Cleared throat, not sure how seeing as there was nothing below the neck to give it wind. Magic, he supposed. Whatever the hell kind of magic this thing swung. "I don't know."

"Awkward." Avaria crossed his arms to his chest. "Do you have a name?"

A smile that said, "You know the answer—why'd you ask?"

Avaria sighed, rolled his eyes. "Right." Stuck in a cave in the Peaks with a head. Stuck in a cave in the Peaks with a head without a body and a name. Had someone told Avaria a week ago where he would be today he would have laughed until it hurt. But—in a wasteland world of demon hounds and demon fowl, who was he to nix the possibility of something this farfetched? "What do you know about the sword?"

Nameless Head perked up. "The sword." Glint in his eyes. "The sword."

Avaria frowned. "Yes—the fucking sword. The Raven's Rage—that thing you begged I find and save not two days ago. What. Do you know. About the sword?"

Nameless Head sneered. "Impatient."

"Things to do," Avaria said. He was not opposed to boxing it across the cave.

"Best do them right," said Nameless Head. "Lest you end up like me."

Clenched teeth. Hiss-sigh. Cough; cold as shit despite the cloak. "Fine."

Nameless Head nodded. "Fine. Where to start...—shut the fuck up. Rhetorical." Fixed its eyes on the ceiling. Threads of... something trailing from its hair. Like a midday sky in summer; not illum, not mirkúr. Just... something else. Strong, old. Avaria hadn't felt it then, back in Ulm. Put a mote of fear in him. Not like that girl of burnt paper flesh, but enough to give him pause. To eke out a fragment of respect.

"Maybe..." Nameless Head fixed its eyes on Avaria. Intent. Hungry. Like a famished wolf. Extended threads of pastel light, caressed his cheeks; grinned. "Maybe I could show you."

Avaria recoiled. Narrowed eyes. "How?"

"Illumancy," said Nameless Head.

Maybe it is *illum.* "My head or yours?"

"I expect implanting... *things* inside your head will be much easier than it is to bring you into mine," said Nameless Head. "As you can see, I'm not entirely here, and it's best to do these things on solid ground."

Avaria sat, crossed his legs. Illumancy. Divination. Not his favorite thing in which to partake; too invasive. But maybe this, whatever Nameless Head was going to show him, might help him make sense of his dreams, whatever it was they were trying to tell him.

"Just... close your eyes." Soft threads against his cheeks. Light kissing his eyelids.

Darkness neither cold nor warm. Just... there. Existent. Sentient?

Whispers, like a million distant, dying screams. Dug his nails into his thighs.

Breathe. Breathe. Breathe...

Silence. The rise and the fall of lungs. Lungs from which the world drew breath.

Light. Light. So much light! Smell of seared flesh—pungent, like ash. Yet sweet like hot honey. What the fuck...

Beach. Starlit ocean and a breeze of salt and sand. Sweet. Cold.

Full-bodied Nameless Head adorned in rags. Looks like him, at least. A second, parallel and draped in red. Regal in a way. Beautiful where Nameless-Head Premier is gnarled and rough. Both bears feathered wings the color of a starless night. The second wields a blade in which infinity exists in tendrils of entwining white and azure light. Beyond them lurks a third thread, faint and dark like coming dusk.

"...You said..." Nameless Head sounds... afraid.

"I said many things," his twin replies. The words are cold.

"You would destroy them," says Nameless Head. "And for what?"

"Reclamation," says his twin. "The only thing that matters. The only thing that *ever* mattered." He draws the blade level with Nameless Head's eyes. "If only you could see..." He heaves a sigh to the salt and sand. *"You will."*

The blade sings.

There is darkness. Foul, like rot and wet earth.

There are screams. Somewhere. Above, below.

His head is empty where it once was not; memories are lost. Somewhere.

Avaria gasped; the cave bloomed.

Nameless Head hovered above him, brow furrowed. "Are

you all right?"

"I..." Avaria massaged the spot between his eyes. "He looked like you—*was* you. A different you... Who...?" Or what. A beautiful man with wings and a blade—*the* blade. What a sight, The Raven's Rage. Gorgeous. Monstrous. "Help me understand."

Nameless Head frowned. "I was hoping *you* might help *me*."

"And how would I do that?" Avaria asked.

"The sword," said Nameless Head. "We find the sword..."

"We find your memories?"

"Something like that—the pertinent ones. I'm not *entirely* void of recollections."

"Great." Avaria coughed. "Fucking thing is supposed to be here in the Peaks, just not sure where. I mean, I have an inkling—I just hope I'm right." Or wrong given everything he'd read, everything he'd eked out of the Virtuoso Archives in the Hall back home. "I don't suppose Rach Na'Schuul rings any bells?"

Another glint in those gray eyes. Wonder. Sorrow. Trepidation.

Knowing.

Avaria sighed. "Fuck."

I WONDER IF they comprehend the nature of this monstrous thing they seek. If they could see what I have seen, see what horrors of memory lurk inside this blade—they would turn back.

If they were sane. If they were not saturated with despair and desperation—they would turn back. But they are all of them broken things. I will intervene. I will speak reason—but it will fall upon deaf ears.

I know—because I have seen this before. Crossed worlds through Pockets, clung to desperation all my own before the terrible truth of everything emerged.

Reclamation is a hydra.

There is no going back.

Only chaos.

SLEEP—HOW MANY CENTURIES since last she'd slept? How long had she been tethered to this leash, this cross-world tug of war? Cat and mouse, hide and seek—stars above, but she wished the game would end. *Knew* that it would end—but where and when and how?

The chill of the Peaks was warm against her flesh, relative to her flesh in the way her lover's hand against her cheek had been so very long ago. It soothed her, gave her pause enough to scent the mountain air—they, all of them, were near. The sad boy and his hounds. The sad girl and her... friend.

She narrowed her eyes. Something more than hounds accompanied the boy—something old and plucked from ruins where her body last had lain. She had an inkling as to what— and it made her seethe.

God-things were deceitful things.

God-things slew their wives.

God-things... had to die.

No—she had left that life behind. In the ruin of a city in the center of a forest dark and dead she had cast aside that guise called Mother Woe. Now, she was nothing—nameless. Free, for nameless things could not be leashed.

"Except," her conscience hissed, *"You are not a nameless thing. You are a thing that fears its name and all that comes attached. The horror and the pain. There is no freedom in ignorance— that is a lie, your lie. Run all you wish but remember this: the truth is never far behind; the guilt will always call you back."*

"I know," she whispered. She closed her eyes; saw not

darkness, but the world—violent, cold, and cruel.

Blood rain.

Chest ache.

Ash.

Quietus in red and white.

"RACH NA'SCHUUL IS dead," said Nameless Floating Head.

"No shit," Avaria said.

"More than just a ruin," Nameless said as they crossed through snow and gloom. No light in the Peaks of Dren. Not anymore. "A... monument."

"Are not most ruins also monuments?" Avaria asked.

"Not the right word, I suppose. More like..."

"An open wound," Avaria said.

"A fissure of regret and shame," said Nameless. "I just can't remember why."

"You will," Avaria said. "I had a dream once years ago. A nightmare, really. In it, something from the darkness spoke: 'The guilt will always call you back.'"

"Profound." Nameless eyed him. "Pray tell, O Savior Mine—what do you flee?"

Avaria's left eye twitched. "None of your concern."

Nameless smiled wryly; squinted. "We're not alone. Look."

Figures, cloaked and hooded, bearing arms. Avaria formed a mirkúr blade and willed his illum wisp to bloom. Eased at faces he'd not seen in years. Rowe, older in the eyes for having danced with and destroyed Te Mirkvahíl; Erath... just Erath.

He trudged ahead, allowed himself a grin—

The world collapsed.

Darkness.

Pain.

SNOW. COLD. COLD like death.

Darkness in the forest save a thread of moonlight.

A body. Small. Shivering. Almost blue. So cold.

Tiny hands clutch snow. Whimper. Weak.

Chaos.

Warmth. Faint. Stronger. Blankets. Swathed in furs to ward away the chill and touch of death. Warmth against his cheek—a hand.

A voice. Incoherent. Calming.

"Breathe, little one. Breathe."

Lungs are weak; wills himself to breathe.

Tiny hand. Fingers searching, clutching. Warm—her hand is warm.

He does not know yet; he drifts between.

He does not know—but *she* knows, knew it when she found him trembling half-dead in the snow.

She pulls him close.

Her baby boy.

"Alone," said a voice. Soft, tired. "You are alone."

"Why?"

"The mountain consumed you," the voice said. "I watched you fall. You broke your neck and died; they left you there, a royal corpse entombed in gloom—now, here you are."

Died. Died? *I'm dead—dead. Fucking dead.* "Where am I?" Darkness. "Who are you?"

"Alone," it whispered. A statement. "Alone..."

Blink.

The world. *A* world. Something. Someplace. Ruin. A city gray and kissed with ice.

"Come."

"Where?"

"She calls. She aches."

"What are you talking about? What is this?"

"Save..." Whimper. Weeping. "Just... save."

Starlight. Air like wet leaves in a winter breeze.

"Save what—who?"

"Mother." Whispers like a song-kissed dying breath, tickling and nipping at his ears. "In the dark of memory... find her."

TATTERED FLESH OF flame and Thread, of time and stars. She is infinite and everywhere, shadow, shade, and silhouette. Her ghoul voice whispers, "Find her."

The darkness screams.

Mausoleum

Erath wasn't sure how far or long she and Rowe and now this floating head had walked. They'd left the latter's corpse companion for the earth; no point dragging dead weight, whoever the hell it'd been. Grim? Sure. Callous? Probably. But such was life—and right now Erath was intent on finding a way out of wherever it was they were.

But curiosity hissed. "Your companion, Head—who was he? Who are you?"

"Haven't the faintest idea," said Head. "In regard to both. People of importance, maybe—he and I both sought a sword, you see."

Erath stopped. Looked at Head. "Sword?"

"Yes," said Head. "Used for stabbing and slicing and—"

"I know what a sword is for. What I'm intrigued by, Head, is the actual sword itself."

Head narrowed his eyes. "You *both* seek The Raven's Rage

as well—why?"

"Dreams," said Rowe. "Nightmares. Somehow, the sword is connected."

"I see." They started on. "I have dreams as well. Memories—an itching where they once were. The blade calls to me. My companion theorized it dwells here in the Peaks. In the ruins of Rach Na'Schuul."

"Isle in the clouds..." Rowe murmured. "A cursed place. Here, somewhere."

Another city in the Peaks of Dren? Erath had never heard of Rach Na'Schuul but she supposed it was possible. The mountains were vast, and nothing really made a lick of sense. Though the way Rowe said an isle in the clouds...

"Did the city... *float* at one time? Sail the skies?"

"It did," said Head. "Until it did not." He sighed, muttered indiscernibly. "Gods fall. Things fall. Inevitable, really."

A city of gods? Fascinating, if such things as gods existed. Erath was skeptical. They called Dren a god, *the* god, *her* god for the simple fact her people bore his name—but there was little if any proof the drenarians were of his hand.

"What makes a god?" she asked. "Or a goddess? Truly, do such things exist or are they merely mortals placed atop pedestals for doing wondrous things?"

"In my experience gods are falsities," Rowe muttered. "Little people adorned in large lies. The most monstrous of things. Gods bring only death."

"A compelling opinion," said Head. "If not mutual. I can't put names to faces, time, nor places but I too have had my share of run-ins with these people playing at goddesses and gods. So much sorrow..."

"Falsities," said Erath, "yet silver-tongued enough to sway the many minds of Harthe." It both disgusted and intrigued her. Words were powerful.

They kept on for a time in silence. Walls of ice and rock grew smooth and etched with symbols unfamiliar to Erath. Symbols which appeared to feast on the pale blue luminescence bleeding from Head. He seemed not to notice, nor did Rowe; or, if they did, neither one said a thing. And what was the essence streaming from Head? Not illum. Not mirkúr.

"What is this place?" Rowe asked.

Erath fell from thought. Before them stood... something. A ruin carved into the whole of a massive cavern with a ceiling through which threads of light crept in. It spanned far and wide; there was no telling how large the ruin was.

"This..." Head hovered, eyes fixed in the ceiling. "This place did not originate within the rock, within the belly of these peaks."

Rowe wrapped her arms around herself, trembling. "This is it," she whispered. She looked at Erath. Fear. Urgency. Realization. "I can feel it tugging at my dreams."

"Rach Na'Schuul," said Head. "A mausoleum where once beauty stood." He floated inward. "Come."

They followed.

THIS STARLIT RUIN kissed with ice evoked a sense of wondrous dread. It was beautiful and horrible; Avaria longed to know it, *ached* to—there was something familiar to this place. This world beyond physicality. Was this The In Between? Where was Equilibrium? Something else, perhaps—but what?

"Mother," he whispered. In the dark of memory, find her. He frowned, trying to riddle out the words, never mind the fact that he was dead. Maybe this was part of the game, the sword testing him—the *world* and *fate* testing him. He passed faceless effigies of winged crystal things, walked beneath archways through which history had come and gone, archways that were history themselves. Directionless but with intent.

"Mother."

Streets like ash-dusted snow. Crystal spires like needles. Death—so beautiful. Lonely.

"You are death." A new voice. Familiar in the way so many unfamiliar things tend to be. Soft. Warm. "Do you see me? Here—just beyond the bridge ahead."

A luminescent silhouette. Tall. Lithe. Beckoning. Avaria made his way; crossed the bridge beneath which rock and water clashed, a violent dance of gray and blue and black. He stopped a sword's length from the master of the voice. Faceless save for eyes like eclipses.

"Who are you? What are you? Where am I?"

"Something. Somewhere," said the silhouette. "Malleable to whatever shape your mind desires—a canvas of radich."

"Radich." A familiar word. Like a memory from a dream. "Possibility."

The silhouette nodded.

"Show me," Avaria said—*willed*. "Show me the truth of things inside my head. Show me the seed from which this all was sown."

The silhouette bowed its head. Snapped its fingers.

Blue sky, sunlight blooming like a wide-eyed babe. A spire in a city in the center of the woods.

She beckoned.

He chased.

HUSH STROKES THE dead boy's cheek. Such broken thoughts. Such a mental massacre—so beautiful. The pain is glorious; it stokes her flames, and she pulls him close.

She whispers—"Find her."

She whispers—"Please..."

She can smell that old scent clinging to his flesh, subtle yet profound, the creeping cold of dark and gloom and woe. The perfume of a broken heart. Hush aches to know.

"Find her."

The darkness of her being thirsts like dying things in a desert. She relents; it consumes the dead boy's flesh and soul, sucks the marrow from his bones and drinks of mirkúr and illum. They are one—the darkness swathes his spirit like a babe; Hush feels... something. His memories bleed, drip through her cognizance like drops of rain—refreshing, slow, so agonizingly slow.

She walks. His task appeals.

Hush hears the sword.

What a song it sings.

WHAT MUST THIS place have looked like once? Before it fell, before the rock and snow consumed it for their own. Erath assumed it had been beautiful; in her experience the most beautiful of things were often fated for horrible ends—her people were proof. Rowe was proof. Steadfast, yet robbed of verve. Of solace by nightmarish dreams—dreams that'd led them here to the corpse of Rach Na'Schuul. Her fingers brushed the wall of a small structure; she winced—a distant wail kissed the depths of her mind. Touched the wall again, longer this time; the wail turned to shrieks and Erath leapt away from the building to the center of the street. What had happened here?

"Don't touch anything," she said to Rowe and Head. "Just... don't, unless you want to hear the dead scream."

Rowe grimaced. "I don't need to touch anything to hear that." She tugged at the collar of her shirt, itched the mark her dance with Te Mirkvahíl had left. "Some days it was bad enough I considered knifing myself." She growled low, pushed her collar into place. "What a life..."

They continued inward. Large crystals bloomed with momentary life, rejuvenated by the luminescence Head left in his wake. Rowe clutched the hilt of her blade with a trembling hand and a grip so tight it made her knuckles white. Erath drew a dagger of her own. Simple steel—the Burn had robbed her of the ability to wield Illum despite the fact it still flowed through her like a constant stream.

"It tugs at me as well," said Head, turning to look at Rowe. "At memories entombed in fog. I have been here before. Many times. Before it fell." A faraway look in his eyes. "This city hates me."

"Why?" Erath asked.

"It just does," said Head. "The why is not yet clear, but the further in we go, the less dammed my recollections are. Answers await in the darkness of this place."

Deep. Deeper yet through the jagged stone and crystal corpse they went. Through the cracks in the cavern ceiling came the distant howl of wind, dulled to a low whistle. They came to rest before the archway of what Erath guessed was once a temple. Weathered, winged effigies yet stood guard, and the jewel in the center of the archway bloomed with faint light.

She looked at Head, at Rowe. "Here?" They nodded. Erath

steeled herself, clutched her dagger tighter. "The sword?"

"Something," Rowe said. "Powerful—feel the energy in the air."

"Odd..." murmured Head. He furrowed his brow, sniffed. He said nothing more, but his expression betrayed intrigue. Memories or not, Erath sensed he knew more about this place than he was letting on—and that did not sit well with her.

They crossed the threshold into the temple; the hair on the back of Erath's neck stood on end; goose pimples rippled down her spine. For the first time since setting off impulsively with Rowe she wondered if she had made a mistake. Maybe it would have been better if she had stayed and moped and mourned in the pale brilliance of the Wisplands. Sure, she would have been lonely, sad, but at least... at least she would have felt... safe.

You idiot, she scolded. *What the hell are you doing here—with Rowe, who looks... not herself, and this melancholy floating head whose every word seems vaguer than the last?* She could practically hear Alor and Leru rolling their dead eyes. Could feel their phantom judgment in the coldness of this place.

"You seek reclamation," said a voice, soft yet resolute. "But there is none here to be found. Only suffering. Only madness."

At the far end of the temple stood a figure shimmering in the gloom. It's tattered, feathered wings were furled against its chest and its eyes shone blue-black like a pair of luminescent bruises. "More than motes have any right to comprehend, for why should suffering be so liberal in its applications?"

Rowe approached, hand still clutched around the hilt of her blade, which she looked increasingly less likely to use the closer she drew to the winged being, whether out of reverence, fear, or something else.

"I've had dreams," Rowe said. "Nightmares, all leading to this ruin buried under rock and snow and ice." She yanked her collar down, flashed the mark around her neck. "I felled the beast who gave me this—why does it yet burn?"

Did Rowe truly believe this thing would know? That it was some sort of all-seer? She stood there, small and insignificant in the shadow of its broken majesty. It unfurled its wings; reached for Rowe and cupped her cheeks with taloned hands.

"Such sorrow."

Rowe touched a taloned hand. "Please..."

Erath started, let out a muffled yelp at a hand on her mouth. A strong arm pulled her into the shadow of the archway. "Quiet," said a male voice, "otherwise she'll hear."

The speaker released her. Erath turned. A familiar face she hadn't seen in years. "Avaria?" Images flashed; Erath's eyes went wide. "Wait... I saw—you were..." She felt dizzy. "You were *dead*."

Avaria shook his head. "No."

"Your neck was broken."

He shrugged. "Illum and mirkúr. I saw darkness, then... I was looking up at the stars from my back." He rubbed his neck. "I *should* be dead but..." Another shrug.

He seemed different than she remembered, but she couldn't say why. The cold of death clung to him—she could feel it standing this close to him, could see it in his blue-tinged flesh.

"You were with that floating head," she said. "Searching for a sword. *The* sword."

"You and Rowe as well by the look of it. Why else would you be in this forsaken hole?" He leaned in. "I know where it is. I don't know why or how, but I can *feel* it, *hear* it. Help me retrieve it, what's left of it, at least."

The Raven's Rage. The blade anathema. She loathed it and its wielder more than anything. Yet she had followed Rowe this far to find the wretched thing. Had thought of reclamation, of the days of yore long before the Burn had ever come to pass. If Rowe, then why not Avaria as well? She'd known him going on a decade after all; they were letter friends as was the term.

"For what do you seek it?" she inquired.

"A chance," he said. "To change everything. Fix things." He hesitated. "Rewrite history itself..."

There it was. "You think that's possible?"

He led her away from the archway. Away from their companions and into the labyrinthine arrangement of the ruin Rach Na'Schuul. Deep, until the city center rose up like a jaw of jagged teeth and the only thing she felt was cold and moderately circumspect about the choices that had brought her here.

Avaria held his arms out wide; a mote of illum bloomed atop his right palm, ascending to illuminate the innards of the stone and crystal corpse. "Rach Na'Schuul was once beautiful," he said. "A utopia. A roost for god-things, kept and hidden by the sky." His expression darkened. "Now it's dead. A mausoleum, as is the fate of all great cities; time waits for nothing. Time is silent vengeance."

"But you think it's possible to alter time?" Erath asked

again. "With The Raven's Rage?" She tried to wrap her mind around the idea. "How... would you even go about doing that? Never mind with the sword—how does one rewrite history?"

"You'd have to ask my mother, General Sel, and Virtuoso Khal. I'm just the errand boy," he sneered, "sent to gather fragments of the blade anathema in hopes reforging it and subsequently wielding it might lead to greener pastures."

Erath smiled sadly, meekly. How to respond? It seemed old habits die hard, old problems lingered like a throng of carrion creatures near a corpse. She reached for his hand, squeezed it gently. "Not much better in my neck of the woods, for what it's worth," she said, and relayed Leru's demise.

"I'm sorry," Avaria said. They walked with measured steps, aimless to the naked eye, but there was obviously intent; the intermittent twitching of Avaria's nose betrayed as such. Could he *smell* the sword or what remained of it, its energy perhaps?

A structure—a tower.

Dark inside; walls infected with a mottling of... sick. Mirkúr, maybe. An inlay in the center of the room—winged things, glorious and talon-handed like the figure whom they'd been confronted by. Beautiful, angelic.

"Dead." The word slipped from Erath's mouth, little more than a hoarse whisper as she noticed, for the first time, the myriad corpses strewn about the room, all preserved in varying states of the decay by the coldness and the gloom. "What happened here?"

"Time," Avaria murmured. He paused, nose to the sky. "The pinnacle. It awaits."

They ascended.

AVELINE KNEW ERATH had withdrawn, stolen away by a dark thing with a silver tongue; she would see to them later. She dropped all pretense of madness and kicked the winged figure away.

"Where is it?" she asked. "The sword. The blade anathema."

The creature smiled wearily. "Your guise might have fooled most, Te Mirkvahíl, but I am not most." The creature tapped its skull lightly. "I know what you are and what you seek." It pointed to Head. "I know what and whom that wretched remnant is as well."

Aveline held her right arm to the side; a mirkúr blade took shape. She placed its length between them. "Then you know

I am relentless in my pursuit," she said. "I have felled queens and kings, razed empires old and new, and this"—she gestured with her free hand—"is but a minor inconvenience. A momentary itch. Where is The Raven's Rage?"

"I too would like to know," said Head. "I don't doubt your claims I'm wretched, not for a moment, for I can feel I am—I *know* I am. But you see, I don't... well, how to put this simply? I don't remember who or what I am."

The creature approached, careful to keep its distance from Aveline. "Do you know who *I* am?" it inquired of Head. It held out its hand. Beads of light streamed outward from its talons, twisting, braiding, blooming to reveal a woman's face. "Do you know who *she* was?" Head trembled. The creature snarled, gripped Head by his hair. "Search your mind, wretch. The answer is there—the guilt will always call you back."

Head whispered indiscernibly. The creature shook him. He murmured, "Sonja."

"*Memoria*," the creature sung, and tendrils of illumination pressed on Head, on the space between his eyes. He howled; Aveline shielded her eyes as the brilliance intensified, grew to a near blinding white light.

Stillness.

Whimpering. A man on his knees, face buried in his hands. "Oh, Sonja..."

Something familiar about him. "Stand," Aveline ordered. "Head—stand."

He obeyed, turned and looked her in the eyes. "What a terrible thing I am," he murmured. "What a parent. Ruination thrice." He reached for Aveline with a quaking hand; his tattered wings hung heavy from his back. "Yet you remain... somehow. The last of the Reshapers."

Aveline curled her lip in a rictus of disgust, placed the blade's length between herself and him. "You abandoned us—"

"He has always been proficient in that respect," the creature said.

Avaline yanked her collar down to reveal the mottling of mirkúr. "Left us at the mercy of this... this..." Memories flashed. Not just a plague envisioned by a random twist of fate. That figure, that face at the far end of a dark hallway the night her beloved Beht fell to ash... *Monster.*" Her blade hand trembled at the coldness of the memory. Bile churned in her gut. "It was born of you—*admit it.* Master of a monstrous thing."

He bowed his head. "Nothing could be more monstrous than I, my dearest Aveline, not even the atrocities my arrogance made manifest. There is a reason they call me Alerésh the Dread."

Aveline narrowed her eyes. "Alerésh? No—you are Varésh Lúm-talé."

Alerésh shook his head. "In another time, on another world, perhaps—but here I am who I am."

Aveline withdrew a step.

"He speaks the truth," the winged thing said—Aveline still was clueless to its name. "He is Varésh Lúm-talé, yet he is not. The being Dren, the first wielder of The Raven's Rage, was once called Varésh too—but it is complicated, maddening to those who fail to comprehend the mechanics of it all. Temporal alteration is so much more than you know—and that is why you will fail."

"Ever the optimist, Oura," Alerésh said. A pep to his words. An edge. "You are no stranger to failure either." He sighed. "What a falsity I am... Did you know, Aveline, the name Varésh Lúm-talé means 'Great Lie?' Of course not— why would you?" A melancholy chuckle as he looked about. "Where is your companion. Where is Erath?"

Oura sniffed the air. Looked at Alerésh and Aveline.

"Sin."

Martyrs

Alf elo nor. One for all.

Nor elo alf. All for one.

Fate was monstrous. Cruel. His mistress. Fate was understanding what he was and always had been at the core. Geph stood atop the hill, overlooking distant Helveden as a midday rain fell heavy, red. His breath clouded, hot with fury, cold with envy. What a wretched engine of destruction he was. He flexed his paws, felt the wet earth; keened his ears, heard the sin buried in the atmosphere. Tasted it.

"One to fall," he whispered. "All to rise." All to fall, one to rise. *She promised.*

How he longed to see his mother.

Geph bayed and the midday trembled 'neath his cry. He waited.

They were coming.

They were hungry.

"Forgive me," he whispered to no one and everyone. "This is requisite." *She* was requisite. *He* was requisite. From entropy, law. From both, balance. He thought of Avaria; they'd not parted well. Geph had chastised his manifesting sinhounds and he saw now he'd been wrong. So *absolutely wrong*. Why leash sin, why keep such beasts at bay when they were a means to peace?

"How very introspective," said a voice in his head. *"It pleases me to know you've seen the error of your ways."* It manifested at his side, an echo of his darkest self—his shadow twin. *"Entombing sin, denying it... that leads only to the manifestation of excessiveness. Of unbounded sin—*false *sin."* It sat back on its haunches, shape billowing in the rain and breeze. *"True sin, Gephorax, is* not, *contrary to belief, evil—and it is vital you remember that. Existence is not black and white, but shades of gray, and only the ignorant believe otherwise. The key is temperance. Be free but understand that everything has limits."*

His shadow twin dispersed.

Geph closed his eyes. *If this is right,* he thought, *then why does it feel so wrong?* He opened his eyes, watched the blood rain soak the distant city like the omen of atrocities it was. His neck prickled with anticipation. The path to peace, to reclamation, he understood, meant sometimes your heart would break; sometimes the right decisions were the hardest ones to make.

"Forgive me," he whispered again, this time to Avaria—and Ahnil. Geph had been there in the woods the night she'd found Avaria as a babe. Even now, despite the rift between them, he could say with all the certainty in his wretched bones that never had he seen a mother more in love.

A change in the wind, a shift in the atmosphere—it was time.

They were hungry.

They were here.

AVARIA HAD BEEN here before in dreams. But the city then had been a ruin. Now? It was a jewel, dark and shimmering, its black streets like deep pools of water swallowing the sky. Towers of midnight kissing the sky like needles drawing thread. He walked, alone, every step suggesting otherwise. He could not see it, smell, nor hear it, but he knew, *felt* there was something in this place. Watching. Waiting. Was it *her*, this figure he had chased here? Something else?

His own words drifted through the air, whispered to him

by the wind. *"Show me the truth of things inside my head. Show me the seed from which this all was sown."* This—what was *this*? What had he meant by that? His dreams, or something more— reality; all of it?

"You return," said a distant silhouette. Nearer, near. Alerésh the Dread. "Again."

Avaria looked about but there was no one save himself for Alerésh to address. "Again... You say that as if we've spoken to one another before." Alerésh did not blink; his stare made the hair on the back of Avaria's neck stand. "Because we *have* spoken to one another before..." He massaged the spot between his eyes. He could feel it was true, yet... "I don't remember doing so. Can't remember where or when or why." He approached Alerésh, stopped and arm's length away. "Are you a memory or something else? Is this The In Between or am I trapped in my own head?"

"We are all of us trapped in our own heads," said Alerésh.

Avaria frowned. "I remember you being vexing. I see that hasn't changed."

Alerésh quirked a smile. "I am, dear boy, what you require me to be. Whether a memory or something more, only time will tell." He gestured to the city. "Banerowos calls you home."

"That city is a lie," Avaria said. "Nothing but the subject of ghost stories. Decidedly *not* my home, whatever you mean by that."

"I mean *exactly* that," said Alerésh, pushing Avaria along. "And Banerowos, for all its mystery and horror, is, I swear to you, decidedly *real*."

"No." Avaria increased his pace into Banerowos as Alerésh trailed. "No. This is just the product of my own loneliness, my fantasizing an adventure while being constantly bound to the Hall. In fact—I'm probably there now, dreaming all of this."

Like smoke, Alerésh was before him. He placed his hands on Avaria's shoulders. "I want you to listen to me carefully," he said. "You, Avaria Norrith, are *physically* dead—your conscious yet remains, but"—a phantom shriek; black lightening snapped across the sky—"time is running out. You need to find an egress from this place."

"Am I stoned beyond all fucking belief?" Avaria asked. "Is that what this is?"

Alerésh growled. "Always were a bit mouthy, weren't you?" He gave Avaria a shake. "This is *real*—as real as Banerowos once was, as real as Ouran'an once was, as real as Hel-

veden is and *will be* if you flee this... this... cognizant collapse.
If this is all in your head, Avaria, that means that I am a part
of you—what reason would I have to lie?"

A good question. Logical. More lightning. Another shriek
and a boom of thunder like a thousand sinhounds howling.

Sinhounds—Avaria hadn't heard from his in... it'd been a
few days at least, since the ruins of Ulm, if his journey to that
place had actually been real. If floating Nameless Head had
been real. If Erath and Rowe and the collapsing earth beneath
his feet had been real and he had, in fact, broken his neck
and—

Myriad distorted images flashed across his mind. Erath? A
ruin deep in the earth. Distorted voices and a tugging sensation at the center of his chest—the sword, The Raven's Rage—

"Fuck." Fuck, fuck fuck. "FUCK." He pushed Alerésh's
hands away. "How do I get out of here?" Shit, how was he
supposed to— "How do I—my body? What do I do?"

Alerésh pointed to the center of the city. "There. You found
the key once before; you can do it again."

Memories, dreams... always so absolutely, irritatingly vague,
Avaria growled to himself. Why could they never be direct?
Why was there always an air of mystery? This wasn't fiction

meant to entertain—this was his existence! He ran for the center of Banerowos, toward the largest of its midnight spires, that tugging sensation in his chest having returned, neither cold nor warm, just simply... there. All of this felt oddly familiar, but there was no way he had lived this all before. No way he had experienced this to some degree at some point in time—was there?

The sky fell dark the closer he grew; gray and purple clouds bloomed like fresh bruises and a throng of shrieks ripped through the silence. So much agony. Was this hell? Had he dreamt himself into an underworld of his own design?

He reached the tower. Broken, weathered by age and rain. He pushed the old doors ajar and slipped inside. Threads of mirkúr clung to the ceiling, walls, and floor like tentacles of something monstrous reaching inward from another world. What had happened here? Fissures in the floor; a shattered floor. Wails and whispers swimming through the air, biting at his ears like hungry flies. *Flee. Save. DIE.*

Avaria started; goose pimples rippled along his flesh and a cold sweat trickled down his brow and cheeks. He stopped in the center of the large anteroom. Alerésh stood beside him, wings yet furled against his chest like a cloak; the feathers though teemed with brilliant light.

"She cannot be allowed in," he said. "She nor her hounds. This is where we part."

Avaria looked at him. "I—"

The tower quaked. "Go!" Alerésh unfurled his wings; a blade of light and darkness formed in one hand. "Please—go! This cannot be for naught. Go!"

Avaria whirled around and bolted down the hallway at the far end of the room. Into the darkness, body trembling; an explosion of light whence he had come. A cacophony of rage and woe. A song, a symphony of sin arrived.

Follow your heart, he chanted mentally; he clung to it like a mantra, the sensation at the center of his chest growing more profound with every step he took, to the point it hurt to breathe. Deeper he ran; deeper he descended, finally coming to a circular chamber illuminated by a single wisp of pale blue light.

"Radich." Was this what he was meant to find? He approached the wisp, reached for it with a trembling hand... hesitated. Pulled away. Withdrew from the chamber and down the hallway to his left. Something about that had seemed far too simple; his proximity to it, the touch of its light had felt wrong.

Inward, downward—when would this all end?

THEY NEAR THE blade for which she thirsts—Hush can feel it with the body not her own. She can feel the dead boy struggle in his mind, feel him flee—he yet resists. She snarls to herself with lips that are not hers. *Breathe,* she urges. Things are as fate wills.

"Come," she calls to Erath. She hungers for the darkness of the woman's soul. Once she has the blade, once she holds The Raven's Rage, Hush decides that she will feed—on everything and everyone. She has never felt such hunger.

She salivates.

They descend.

She can smell the secrets kept by Rach Na'Schuul.

Her stomach roars.

WHAT DOES IT matter if this thing kills her? Aveline thought of Erath's disappearance. *I would have done it myself; I would see her born anew—I would see them all returned once I possess The Raven's Rage and rewrite time.* She sighed; inner voices scolded her. She chastised herself mentally and could practically feel

Alor whacking her in the back of the head for such a thought. *For you, Alor. For you, I will save her from this thing that stole her from my sight. For you, I will give her a choice.*

She followed Alerésh and Oura as the latter tracked their quarry's scent. Through the corpse of Rach Na'Schuul they went. Ruined houses, broken shops, dead groves peppered all about, now ruled only by dead crystals void of color. Nothing here, Aveline realized, held color. Not the colors of life nor the colors of death and everything that followed. Just endless grays that saw fit to trick the eye. Strange. Unnerving. As if this place were somehow trapped in time. Aveline cocked an eyebrow pensively—was that even possible?

She held her thought as Rach Na'Schuul trembled. The cavern ceiling cracked, sending shards of ice and rock hurtling toward the city. Aveline, Alerésh, and Oura charged ahead, dodging debris as best they could, finally coming to a maw in the street in which they would take shelter.

"It stirs the city," Oura said. "The sin that stole your friend—look."

Aveline peeked out at the city. Gossamer threads of energy swam about; spirits manifested. Rach Na'Schuul moaned. She ducked back into hiding. "What is this? What is happening?"

"Unwilling martyrs rise to keep their tomb," Alerésh murmured. He closed his eyes and sighed. "I remember this moment as if it happened yesterday." He gripped Oura's hand; she yanked it free. "This is The Fall."

"We must hurry," Oura said. She motioned they withdraw.

Aveline first, then the other two. Through ghosts and gray they went. So many screams; Aveline's skull ached, longed to explode. She could hear their rage and suffering in her mind, could feel it in her bones and it made her want to die for it reminded her of home—of the fall of Ouran'an. Of Beht and Jor. Of everyone and everything that she had ever known and loved.

They pushed into the city center, found themselves surrounded, set upon by spears of twisting light and dark. Aveline parried with her mirkúr blade, sent the blast of energy upward, watched it take a spirit in the chest. It stung in her heart to have done so; things dead should not have to suffer the living.

"Can't you reason with them?" she asked of Alerésh and Oura. "They're your people, are they not?"

Oura's wings shimmered with light; a barrier pushed back against the onslaught. "The dead cannot be reasoned with," she said, "especially not those twisted by her song." A glint in her eyes. "Songs... Sing with me, Alerésh. Sing as once our people sung to Mother Moon and Father Sky."

"We will give you time enough to run," Alerésh said to Aveline. He pointed to the remnant of a large tower infected with shattered crystals. "There."

"High above," Oura added. "In the heart of Rach Na'Schuul." She gripped Aveline's arm, pulled her close so that their noses nearly touched. "Do what is right. Fight your selfishness—break the cycle."

Aveline pulled away. "I will do what I must."

Their wings shimmered; they began to sing. The spirits shrieked. *Just wait. Just wait.* So many ghosts. Endless. Hungry. The barrier faltered; threads of light fell like shards of glass.

She ran as the spirits converged. Felt the mirkúr flowing through her, cold, desperate; she called the shadows of this place and they accepted her. Like smoke, she stood before the tower archway, away from the chaos. She gave a half-second glance back at the mass of wailing energy. Then, she stepped inside.

* * *

AVARIA TOUCHED DOWN in... an anteroom? He looked about—surely he had been running *down* the stairs, but this... felt like he was back to where he started. He conjured a wisp of light. The chamber was dark, but his light offered a modicum of clarity, enough that he could walk without tripping. The air smelled of dust and dirt and was thick enough Avaria could almost imagine it parting around him as he went.

"What the..."

This place was massive.

"It might behoove us to split up and explore."

Avaria started at the voice, whipped around. "Alerésh?"

"Maybe?" said Maybe-Not-Alerésh. *Definitely* not Alerésh. He was garbed in black, and his flesh bore tattoos that shone with the same blue light—radich—that'd come from the wisp in the chamber somewhere upstairs. From the tattoos manifested three wisps of illumination. "Considering the size of the spire and the clock we're running against would you not agree we should split up?"

Clock? Avaria smacked his forehead. "Right. Clock—are we talking about the same clock? Are *you* talking about the same thing as the, uh...—your *twin* was talking about?"

Definitely-Not-Alerésh shrugged. "The mind tends to—

oh, what's the phrase? Fuck things up on occasion. Especially when one—such as yourself—is in a bad way." He narrowed his eyes. "What did you do?"

"I died," Avaria snapped. "I *fucking died* and now I'm trying to keep my mind from being devoured by some... thing. I have no idea what's going on; I need to escape. Somehow."

"Sure," Definitely-Not-Alerésh said. "Sure. Look. I'll take the third and fourth floors, you take the second. We'll meet back here once we're done and relay our findings. There should be something here that can help."

"Right. Fine." Avaria watched Definitely-Not-Alerésh ascend the corkscrew. He manifested a mirkúr blade and followed suit, his newish companion becoming little more than a glowing dot as Avaria reached the second-floor landing and started into the chamber on his left. His own wisp ascended to the ceiling, casting its brilliance over the room. It was adorned with myriad bookshelves, each packed to capacity with leather-bound tomes, and in the corner was a desk, it, too, overflowing with various texts. It was the engraving on the wall at the far end of the room, though, that drew Avaria further in.

"A raven," he murmured. This memory or dream or whatever of his, these ruined cities and winged people... there was something more to it than that which currently met his eyes.

He pressed into the adjoining chamber, at the center of which stood the stone effigy of a giant bird, its feathers fluctuating midnight to snow white and back. It was beautifully hypnotic, so much so Avaria almost failed to notice the body lying limp at the statue's base. He rushed to its side. He wasn't sure who it was or what had happened to them, but they were still alive, though barely just, their breathing labored. Avaria rolled them gently onto their back and gasped.

"You're... me?"

His twin replied weakly in a language Avaria once again could not understand and allowed Avaria to help him to his feet. They were twins only in the face. Everything else was different. Tattoos not unlike Definitely-Not-Alerésh's peeked out from the sleeves and collar of his robe, glowing faintly, and his dark hair was pulled back into a series of thin braids. He rolled his shoulders back, then motioned for Avaria to follow him back the way he'd had come.

They were silent as the newcomer led Avaria back to and up the corkscrew stairway. For a man who'd looked near death just minutes ago he was unnaturally alert, his movements fluid, graceful. There was purpose in his steps and Avaria wondered where they were going, who the stranger was if not an echo of himself.

"Nothing atop," Definitely-Not-Alerésh said, descending toward them. "Silent as the…" He rushed to the man, embracing him. The gesture was returned with enthusiasm and the two conversed in their strange language.

"Who is he?" Avaria asked.

"A friend," Definitely-Not-Alerésh said. There was a sadness underneath his smile. "A friend long dead but ever present in this place of memory. Please meet Jor Dov'an."

The man, Jor, bowed his head to Avaria and he did the same in return. Jor tensed his jaw, looked toward the chamber on their right. There was apprehension dancing in those purple eyes. Fear, too, and… was it anger?

"Is he all right?" Avaria asked.

"He will be." Definitely-Not-Alerésh started toward the chamber. "Come."

Avaria trailed them, blade extended. He hadn't liked the look on Jor's face and had liked Definitely-Not-Alerésh's reply even less. He hoped they were going in the right direction, that he would soon find the key to his egress from his labyrinthine mind, but who could tell in a place like this, in the twisted dreams and maybe-memories of a man so desperate for adventure, for escape, and—

Avaria's breath caught in his throat as the wisp light revealed a dozen or so corpses strewn about the room. Blood stained the polished floor. The corpses' eyes were a sickly white with threads of what Avaria guessed was mirkúr twisting aimlessly about. He swallowed, clutched his blade tighter. What was this horrible place he had fallen into?

I died, he recalled. *And my body...* Dread crept through him as the realization dawned—his dreams and memories were bleeding together with whatever *thing* now wore him like a suit. This phantasmagoria would not release him unless he fought.

They crossed to the other end of the chamber and into the room beyond. More corpses. More blood. Walls and pillars infested with wispy tendrils of mirkúr, with a pulsating, thickening membrane. Mirkúr, too? Avaria swallowed the urge to retch—at everything.

"Slow," Definitely-Not-Alerésh said. There was worry in his tone, in the crease of his brow. He asked something of Jor—at least, Avaria thought it was a question—and Jor offered only a tiny nod. "Be on your guard."

As if Avaria had needed instructing in that regard. They continued through a network of hallways, their steps hastening as they went, before they finally came to rest in what looked to be a bedroom. At the far end of the room stood a red-haired woman and a blond-haired man, back-to-back, eyes darting about. Repressed instinct—Avaria wasn't sure if it was his—bid he run to them, but Jor blocked his path with his arm.

Jor shook his head and pointed to the shadows on the wall, cast by the wisp light.

"Vultures?" Avaria asked. "Sinhounds?"

Jor nodded. His tattoos bloomed beneath his robe and an illum longsword took shape in his hand. Definitely-Not Alerésh did the same and the pair advanced into the room at a walk, Avaria at their heels, itching to imbed his dagger in whatever thing saw fit to provoke him. They reached the man and woman and the shadows struck. Avaria sidestepped, thrusting his dagger clumsily into the demon nearest him, but the blade had no effect and simply passed through his quarry's smokey form.

"Run!" Definitely-Not-Alerésh ushered Avaria out of the chamber. Avaria obeyed, but not without a prolonged glance at Jor, who shouted in his foreign tongue.

They sprinted back the way they had come, their steps haunted by the distant shrieks of demons as Jor gave them time to flee. They descended to the base of the tower and burst out into the night in time to see the fog encroaching from the woods. Without hesitation they turned tail and bolted for the trees beyond.

Avaria was not sure how long they had been running when they finally stopped to catch their breaths. He looked at Definitely-Not-Aleresh. "Your name—what is it?"

"Now? Varésh," he said. "Why do you ask?"

Avaria frowned. "Just curious." He cracked his neck. "I don't understand anything that's going on. All of this is..." He gestured wildly. "I've walked The In Between before, and this—this is something more."

"The mind is a dangerous place. Quite disordered, as you can see." His expression darkened. "Especially when your dreams and memories braid together with those belonging to a monster."

That was an understatement if ever Avaria had heard one, and it only served to chill him further—he had confirmation. Disordered didn't begin to describe the situation. His thoughts returned to Jor. "Your friend—"

Varésh shook his head sadly and Avaria understood. But what had he witnessed? His heart stung despite his best effort to remain indifferent. *Why* did it hurt? He massaged the spot between his eyes. Hopeless. Desperate. Confused. He looked at Varésh. "Am I going to escape this place?"

Varésh pointed straight at the darkness of the wood. "The key. You found it once before. You'll find it again—you'll know it when you do."

So Avaria went. Alone. Cold. Through a dark wood of error. Screaming trees. Bleeding earth. Whispers kissed his ears, promised death, begged for torture. Ached for release. Trembled. Still, he walked, hugged himself tight. Thought of nothing but freedom from this hell. Followed his heart.

A clearing. A tree greater than all others. Corpses swung, danced the dance of death. Gods, so many bodies. He looked about—withered waltzers by the hundreds. More. Oh, gods...

Back to the great tree. To the figure standing at its base. Garbed in black. Eyes black as night. Skin pale and cracked. Like that girl of burnt paper flesh; not her. Different. Cold, but... cold in the way intense heat feels on one's skin. He wilted underneath her stare.

"This place is mine," she said. Voice like serpents hissing rain. Angry. Scared.

Stomach churned bile. Sour taste on his tongue. Hand shook, still clutched his blade. He placed its length between them. "This place is *mine*—let me out." He took one step toward her. Furrowed his brow. Rictus. Growl. "Let. Me. *Out.*" Called out with his mind. *Envy. Pride. Wrath.*

"They'll not come," she said. "They are not yours."

"My head, my hounds," Avaria said. Hot with rage, with desperate intent. Distant howls. He grinned. "See?"

She swallowed, pressed her back to the trunk of the massive tree. "*Please.*"

Like smoke, Avaria was before her, blade to her chest.

"You will doom them all," she whispered. Tears streamed from her abyssal eyes. "If you leave. If you leave the temperance disappears. *Please!*" She grabbed him by his shirt. "*Please... I just...*" She sunk into the blade, wept into his chest. "So tired..."

The forest shrieked.

"Again." Her speech was soft. "Here we go... again."

Light exploded.

Burned. Gods, it burned.

Avaria screamed.

HUSH SCREAMS. SOMETHING in the depths of her being has been violated. Desecrated. She falls to the floor, writhes in the body not her own. Erath tends to her frantically. All Hush can do is weep. Howl as the body not her own rends itself from the inside out and energies bleed and flee. Twist and braid and slither through the ruined ceiling of this place.

She lays there, dying. This was not foreseen—but this is fate, and Hush does as fate wills.

She dies.

AVELINE FOUND THEM on the topmost floor of the tower. She dispersed her blade; she breathed a sigh of relief at Erath, hands covered in blood but otherwise fine. She glanced at the corpse, her right eye twitched. It was Alerésh's companion, the one they had left behind. She shouldn't have been disturbed by it considering the numbers of bodies her vultures had stolen and worn, and yet she could not stomach the mess. She doubled over and retched.

"Are you all right?" Erath asked.

Aveline stood tall, wiped the bile from her mouth. "Fine.

Could ask the same of you." She nudged the corpse with her foot. "Wasn't actually him, whoever this *thing* claimed to be. It was..." She shook her head. "I don't know what it was. Dangerous."

"Avaria Norrith," Erath said. Her voice trembled. "Prince of Ariath. A friend."

Aveline sighed, pulled Erath into an embrace. How many more people would this poor girl lose before all was said and done? "Shit," she whispered. Half to play the part, half to actually... mourn? "How could we have not noticed? The *Prince of Ariath*. What a wretched journey this has been..."

Truly—what a wretched journey, what a wretched life these last however many thousand years, however many centuries Aveline had walked this world alone. Was Oura right—was failure all fate had in store for her? She glanced past Erath to a shattered blade encased in brilliant pale blue light. There it was. She pulled away from Erath and approached the sword.

"The Raven's Rage," she said. "As I dreamt." She held her hand to the light, manipulating it with her fingers. "So much possibility." She'd not tasted of radich in ages; it was sweet, its phantom vapors like honey on her tongue. "Rewrite history with the blade anathema—what do you think?" She had given her word—a choice. "Erath?"

The drenarian approached, stopped a few feet from Aveline.

"I don't know."

Somehow, Aveline had expected that. She smiled softly. Thought of Alor. Of Beht and Jor. A lump formed in her throat. Urgency and desperation gradually melted away, replaced instead with sorrow. How absolutely bittersweet. "Me neither. In fact..." She heaved a ragged sigh, fought back tears. "We should destroy it—once and for all. Such power should not exist. It is far too dangerous, far too tempting, and I have seen what sin does because..." She trailed off. "War does terrible things." Truth to hide her lie.

Erath nodded. "How?"

"The same way it was wrought," Aveline said. She placed a hand on Erath's shoulder. "We take it to Dren."

"TO... DREN." ERATH felt dizzy among other things. "To Dren because..."

"He wrought The Raven's Rage," said Rowe. She chewed her lip; Erath could sense she was keeping something from her. "He... fuck. Dren is the one responsible for the Burn,

Erath. He was the wielder of the blade."

"No." Erath shook her head. "No, why would he—*no*. Who told you this?"

Rowe explained what had transpired down below after Erath had left. She felt sick. Betrayed. Was that all her people had ever been—martyrs for a madman's desires? She tensed her jaw. "*If* Dren is even still alive, how do we find him—and can I kill him once The Raven's Rage is dust?"

"The Wisplands," Rowe said. So much guilt drawn across her face.

"You and I are going to have a *long* talk once this is all said and done," Erath snarled. She looked to Avaria's corpse. Just ash and a twist of mirkúr. Was that what happened to his kind, those able to wield mirkúr, when they died? She wasn't sure.

"Let's go."

GEPH WEPT AT her feet. She had died peacefully—they all had, with grins stretched wide across their faces. It horrified him; the joy of corpses wormed its way inside his mind, tattooed itself to Geph so he would never forget what had transpired here this day—what *he had done* this day.

At least, he thought, *her end was not my doing.* He could never have lived with that—murdering Queen Ahnil. Everyone else? His soul would bear the weight, the guilt, profound as it already was. He had no other choice.

"You did well, Gephorax," his shadow twin whispered.

If by 'well' you mean I destroyed a city, Geph thought, *then yes—I did.*

"From entropy, law. From both, balance. Stick to the path, Gephorax."

Geph pressed his nose to Ahnil's cold cheek. "Forgive me..."

He withdrew from Helveden. The city burned. The dying sang.

But Geph sang louder.

Time

Time was cruel. She found them in the corpse of Rach Na'Schuul; their final song hung heavy in the stunted air. Dead air. Oura had been good, always good; Varésh Lúm-talé had been a lie, always a lie. "Alerésh," she sneered. "As if you could ever have lived up to his stolen name. As if you could ever have been Alerion." She took his light, took his radich for her own. So delicious. She wreathed Oura in darkness, swaddled her in shadows; delivered her from hell, for such a timeless place as this could only be described as eternal damnation.

"Hell is a place of one's own making," she whispered. An echo out of time, those words. She breathed the stale air. "I see. Hush is what you call yourself now. What do you seek? What madness drives you?"

Shift in the atmosphere. Breath on her neck. She turned.

"You're here." Horror of shadow, flame, and stars. Limp

wings trailing like a tattered cloak. It reached for her with a quivering hand, bore into her with eyes like tarnished coins alight. "Luminíl..."

Luminíl furled her wings against her chest and hissed. "Monster."

Hush recoiled, whimpered. "Monster... yes, but..." Ragged breath. "For you, Luminíl. All for you. No—" Scratched her eyes, snarled, wailed. "For them. For all. Deliverance. I need you." Absolute certainty. "Badly. So... *badly*."

"No one *needs* anything," murmured Luminíl. Half a lie— right? "But you—you need sleep." Eternal. Dreamless. "*I* want to sleep. So long since last the darkness kissed my eyes. Every death, a lie. Every life, perpetual agony—and *you* are to blame."

She raised a hand to Hush—

Fire in her chest. Burning.

Cold. So cold.

Not again.

Hush screamed. Reached for Luminíl.

Quietus in ruin.

Hell.

* * *

Snow.

Silence.

Helveden was a corpse. The clouds hemorrhaged; Avaria walked the dead streets. Crows picked at lifeless flesh, pulled eyes from sockets, tongues from mouths. Spires stood like jagged teeth. None of this was right—how long had he been gone? What had happened here? Was any of this real? He pressed himself to think, to remember—a dark forest, girl of black and woe.

"Hello?" An echo in the stillness of death.

He remembered dying in the Peaks. Sort of. Remembered *learning* he had died. Traversed his labyrinthine mind. Walked ruins, fled monsters. Any of this—what was *any* of this?

"HELLO?"

Shimmers. Twists of light and shadow. Avaria cocked an eyebrow. Distant screams kissed his ears. Distant, yet so very near. He frowned; fear crept through him like a frozen river thawing. Slow, rushing. He pushed through Helveden, what was left. Raced for the Bastion. *Dream*, he urged. *Just let this be a dream.*

A nightmare. Had someone else made it to The Raven's Rage before him? Fuck, had *he* obtained the blade and done something catastrophic, so profound he couldn't remember? *Wish you were here, Geph.* Longhound could always make sense of madness.

Figures in the distance. City draped in fog. Whispers on the wind. Avaria gave chase, called to the phantoms—no answer. Through charred groves and splintered courtyards. Thick rain, snaps of light. To the Bastion, through defiled gates. Streaks of... blood. Threads of mirkúr twisting, tickling ruined stone, drifting.

They beckoned from the egress.

Avaria indulged.

TIME WAS A peculiar thing. Abhorrent, really. Time disgusted Dren; he disgusted himself. He deserved worse than this, jailed within the Wisplands of the peaks that bore his name. So much worse than luxury when his children dwelled in woe, forsaken by the sunlight—forsaken by their father. Intent was blinding. Intent was fueled by arrogance, and arrogance by intent. He sighed.

"What a thing," he mused. "What a lie I am. Living whilst my children think me dead. I *should* be dead—worse than dead. Yet here I am..." He sighed. Waited for the myriad voices in his head to snicker, snarl, and whine. That was the thing about imprisonment—it drove the mind insane. Snuck in pictures of a previous life, a twisted knife in a rotting wound. Dren had been someone else once. Better by the looks of it, though "better" was subjective. Relative, rather; the person he *had been* was prickish in his own right—just not to the genocidal degree for which Dren dwelled in shame.

He withdrew from the darkness of his cave, the ruin of a temple crafted in his name. Wisplight kissed his flesh; it stung his eyes and he looked away to a copse of trees, leafless, dead. Dead, like so many of his children. He narrowed his eyes, watched two silhouettes emerge. Emotion roiled through the air, anger, fear, and grief. Confusion. They were coming toward him, coming *for* him—a drenarian and the creature called Te Mirkvahíl.

And they were wielding something monstrous. Dren felt sick; his stomach gurgled. The Raven's Rage had come home to roost. He sucked in his breath, steeled himself as best he could, and greeted them with open arms. They stopped at the base of the crumbling, snow-covered stairs. In Te Mirkvahíl's eyes he saw guilt and sorrow. In the drenarian's, rage. Hatred. She knew.

"Rowe." He nodded to Te Mirkvahíl. To the drenarian, he bowed his head. "Erath." He was lost for words, and his breath caught in his throat. Unexpected. "Erath, I..."

"Alive," Erath hissed. "Alive all this time..." Dren could practically feel the heat of her fury in her words. "Rowe told me something interesting. She told me *you're* responsible for the Burn. That *you* wrought this cursed fucking blade..."

No words. What was Dren to say? What could he say that would erase years of pain? That would rectify the monstrous consequences of the Burn? He heaved a sigh, and his guilt felt like a thousand thorns biting his heart. "Yes."

Cold wind and silence. Te Mirkvahíl looked from Dren to Erath and back. Ironic such a monstrous thing as her would mediate whatever conversation was to take place, though maybe not considering what a monstrous thing it was that Dren had done. *We are monsters,* he thought. He looked at Erath, surprised she hadn't tried to kill him yet; she deserved to, and he sensed she longed to.

"Why?" she asked. "All of it—why?"

Truth. No sense in lies. Look where those had gotten him. Look where those had *always* gotten him. "Reclamation is a complicated thing. An undertaking often fueled by desperation." Again, he sighed. He approached them, dragging his dead wings through the snow. "The blade was to be the key, the means to unlock the doors to the Temporal Sea."

"Temporal alteration..." Erath murmured. "It's *possible*?"

Dren nodded. "Very much so—but dangerous. Destructive. The price is often far too high, so it took the Burn for me to learn. To save what has been lost, one first must destroy what is yet to be lost, do you understand?" He searched her eyes. "To save this world, I was going to destroy it—but I failed."

Silence reigned. Dren waited for either of the women to respond, though he doubted Te Mirkvahíl would lest she betray her lie.

"There is hope, however small it may be, to reverse the Burn," Dren said, "and the key lies here"—he held his arms out wide—"in the Wisplands. I know because there is one amongst you who was spared that day. He never made mention of it, walked as the rest of you walked in solidarity. His character kept his freedom secret. Fenrin was and is the king of kings."

"He was here that day..." Erath looked about. "Something about the wisplight."

Dren nodded. "Speak with him if you wish." He eyed the blade at Te Mirkvahíl's waist. "What will you do with it?"

"Destroy it," she said. "As you made it, so must you *un-make* it."

"Gladly." Did he mean that? Such power in The Raven's Rage, such potential... He shuddered. Gestured to Te Mirkvahíl to bring the blade. She approached; he took it from her, felt the energies permeate his flesh, the entirety of his being. He felt *awake* as images flashed across his mind—The Raven's Rage had indeed come home to roost.

Memories across the span of time. Across realities not yet always mine. So many worlds. The illum network was a wondrous thing. Mysterious in its full potential, but clear enough to Dren to understand what he had seen. To remember who he had been, was, and always would be—and it made him sick. With guilt. With possibility. *Radich, my old friend...* The sword rose from Dren's hand, hovered as he wreathed it in mirkúr and radich. Soft threads of energy streamed along the blade—and gradually it fell to mist. Gone. Dead.

And Dren felt weak. Tired. He sat down in the snow and closed his eyes.

"It is done," he said. "Go. Leave me to my end—it *is* coming."

"We loved you," Erath said. Such sorrow, such pain. "But we were wrong."

Dren said nothing, only listened to the screaming silence as Te Mirkvahíl and Erath turned and walked away.

Please, he thought, *let this have been the right thing to do.*

He opened his eyes to the barren, snow-draped waste...

and conjured The Raven's Rage.

So. That had been it. Dren was alive and The Raven's Rage had been destroyed far more easily than Erath would have imagined possible given the mystique behind the blade anathema. Somehow it all seemed... anticlimactic.

She eyed Rowe as they trekked through snow and trees. Neither had said a word since leaving Dren to perish in his ruin. Erath wasn't sure what she wanted to say. What she was sure of, however, was that she wanted an explanation from Rowe—about everything. How had she known Dren was alive? What about Rach Na'Schuul? The more she thought on everything, the more she felt like there was far more that Rowe was keeping from her. Where had she gone after the war, after felling Te Mirkvahíl, and if the demon was well and truly dead then why did vultures and hounds still run amok? Why was Leru dead?

Rowe halted. She looked exhausted, and if anything, the mark around her neck had grown worse. Threads of mirkúr webbed out of her garb and up her neck.

"Over..." she murmured. "All of it—over..." She leaned against a tree, slid down the trunk and sat in the snow. Silent tears streamed down her cheeks. "You deserve the truth..."

ROWE WAS DEAD. Had been all this time. Erath was numb. She looked at this *thing*, this monstrous *thing* that wore the image of her friend, wore her flesh as if it were a coat in and out of which she slipped with ease. Her chest was heavy, and her thoughts were shrieking.

"I loved her, you know," Te Mirkvahíl said softly.

"Who?" Erath asked. "Rowe?"

"Alor," said Te Mirkvahíl. Shadows twisted round her form; reshaped her into someone Erath swore she'd seen before, had known a time ago.

"..." Erath clapped a hand to her mouth. "*Aveline...?*" What was going on? So many names within names. It was getting hard to keep up. "You—you're Te Mirkvahíl." A statement she had meant as a question, though she supposed it didn't matter; the truth stood before her, broken, sad. She thought back to Alor, to her death at the hands of Ariathan soldiers and their blades. Something in her ticked, clicked, snapped—everything made sense. "Your war was in her name."

Aveline nodded. "I felt at peace with Alor. At ease, so much so the import of my undertaking waned. I..." She breathed deeply, heaved a sigh. "Felt I could finally let go of what had come to pass; I had accepted my people were gone. That my husband and son were gone." She reached for Erath's hand, squeezed it tightly. "You were a tremendous part of that. You were my friend, Erath..."

Erath let the words sink in, let them swim and slosh and permeate her soul. Friend. What a strange word, that. Friend. Friends. So foreign after all these years, coming from the mouth of... this. Aveline. "Time is monstrous."

"People are more so," Aveline murmured. Erath could practically taste the shame, the regret in her words. What a sorry, lost creature. What sorry, lost creatures they both were. "Do you recall what you asked me on our ascent? To find one-self by losing hope?"

Erath nodded. "Having an epiphany?"

Aveline nodded.

"Don't need you to tell me," Erath said. She thought she understood well enough by looking upon Aveline—Aveline as she truly was. In doing so, Erath realized she had never felt more lost. More... fragmented.

"Will you walk with me?" Aveline asked.

"No," Erath said. "I..." She what? "I'm going to speak with Dren." What a stupid idea. What a stupid instinct. "Just... something."

She pulled her hand from Aveline, turned to walk away. Paused. Turned back and pulled Aveline to her. There was a lot to work through, but... "Come find me in Nil-Illúm. We'll figure things out, somehow."

Aveline pulled back, flashed a melancholy smile. It faded; her eyes darkened. "I need you to know, Erath. Leru's death— that wasn't me."

Erath nodded; a chill crept through her. If not Aveline, then who? What?

"Be safe."

"You, too."

They turned from one another
and went their separate ways.

* * *

THROUGH THE BASTION courtyard, where for every corpse there buzzed a thousand flies, or the deafening sound implied. Avaria swallowed the urge to retch and continued inward, measured steps hastening with every lifeless face he passed. Eyes burnt out; flesh charred. Dying breaths lingering in the foul air, as if spirits struggling for release but tethered to this hell. Was this a nightmare? An alternate reality? What had happened in the Peaks? What had happened in *his own mind*?

He pushed the battered Bastion doors ajar; the anteroom was cold and ruined, stained with gore and kissed with wispy threads of mirkúr rippling in the air like tentacles.

"Hello?" Stupid. Foolish. Whatever had done this might still be lurking—but he needed answers. He needed *someone, something* to answer, to let him know if he was dreaming or awake.

Were you sleeping, boy, what then? Would you will yourself awake? Would you will yourself awake to find you'd actually been awake this whole time? What then?

The voice sent a chill up Avaria's spine; goose pimples rippled along his flesh. The voice sounded distant yet so very near, ethereal yet whole. Something in between.

"Show yourself and find out," Avaria said. He willed a blade to take form... but neither light nor shadow granted his request. What was going on?

Laughter. Hissing. Giggling cackle shriek. The song of a dying bird. The horrible sound pierced his ears; he felt blood trickling, creeping down his jaw. Heard the cacophony in the depths of his mind like a symphony of dead and dying monstrous things. Avaria clutched his ears and screamed.

Silence. Fog and a Bastion anteroom devoid of gore. Pristine, as beautiful as Avaria had ever seen it. A silhouette atop the raven inlay, lithe and cloaked in feathered wings. It neared—Avaria had seen this thing before.

"Floating Head..." he murmured.

The figure smirked. "One of many names bestowed upon me, yes. Call me BzZzzzz." He unfurled his wings, feathers shining like a cloudless midnight sky. "Time is a peculiar thing. A wretched thing. A peculiarly wretched thing, dear boy, as can be the mind. Wondrous and terrible."

"What is this?" asked Avaria. Was he going mad? Was this hell?

"The calm before the storm," said BzZzzzz. "Monsters

walk the earth and sing their songs of ruin. The world falls in tempo with their stride. Or will. But you must wake. Push through memory and take the hands of Time."

Avaria massaged the spot between his eyes. "None of that makes sense." He looked about the anteroom. "Where did all the bodies go?"

"Like I said, time is peculiarly wretched." Such melancholy in those words, in that stormy stare.

Avaria felt his stomach drop. "All of... that..." He gestured at the vacancy. "It was real, wasn't it? Something happened to Helveden. To..." Urgency erupted; he pushed past BzZzzzz. "Mother! Norema?" Adrenaline like a gushing wound. "Virtuoso Khal?"

He charged through the fog. Screams and whispers rose from nothingness to omnipotence. Stumbled. Vision blurred. Bile churning in his gut, mind waxing and waning.

Emptiness dilating. Throne room of horror. Monsters ripping limbs and rending flesh. Hounds of sin and flame and nightmare grins.

"Mother!"

Maddened grin ripped wide across her face; eyes like burning coals. She cleaved her acolytes—

Then by Norema's blade she fell.

And by the hounds, Norema's head was severed at the neck and her body fell limp and flopping with whatever dark power the hounds possessed.

So much agony. So much screaming. Heartache. Betrayal—by the throne stood Geph. Watching. Silent. Eyes alight with flames the color of a midday summer sky.

"Forgive me," the longhound *sinhound bastard fucking monster* mouthed, the cadence of his sorrow and regret muffled, almost choked to silence as the fog returned and everything went dark.

HUSH LOVES STREAMS. They remind her of the illum she brandished long ago. Gentle, beautiful, but dangerous when provoked. Much like someone she loved so long ago.

She senses a woman, the Reshaper, so she turns.

"I knew you would be here," said Aveline. "You reek of mirkúr. Of temporal rot. What are you?" The trees moan. "Hold that thought—those would be the hounds."

Hush gives a weary smile. "They are coming for you—but not in the way you think. Hubris... is amusing when it comes from things who play at god." A dark blade takes shape in her hand. It holds form as the hounds erupt from the trees—a good sign.

Aveline drinks them in. Hush can see it in her eyes—she has caught her unprepared. Dilated pupils unmask fear.

"You haunted us in Rach Na'Schuul," says Aveline. "Hunted. What are you?"

"Timeless." Hush strokes the ears of the hound nearest her. "Some have called me Mother Sin. Others, Devourer of Vice. Even a small handful have called me goddess... It's a matter of perspective, really. But the simplest of answers is—I'm the greatest quisling of them all."

Aveline arches an eyebrow at that.

Hush takes one step toward her—and Aveline flinches. "How weary you must be... Lonely. To have walked the world alone for all these years... I expect it all begins to blur." The hounds entomb her with their size. Hush holds her dagger toward Aveline. "I can help you though—and helping you, helps me. Do you understand?"

Aveline's eyes are white beneath her sway. Hush wonders if she feels it on her neck, the breathing of the hounds—the flimsy barrier between their hunger and her flesh. Or perhaps the dagger entering her chest, or the grass beneath her back as

Hush lays her gently by the stream.

"Forgive me." Hush isn't sure to whom she is appealing; it simply sounds like the proper thing to say for having a killed a woman entranced.

She rips the blade from Aveline's silent heart. "They told me, whispered through the shadows you would come. Hounds are loyal beasts—especially to the cloth from which they all were cut. They call me mother and I love them so."

She places a hand atop Aveline's chest and draws her mirkúr through the wound. Imbibes her memories and dreams, her sorrow and her joy. She had a family once, a husband and a boy.

A tear streams from Hush's eye. It's been millennia since last she's cried. She leans in close, whispering, "I will save you all."

Hush rises; from the glade she goes—she has a blade to steal.

The hounds bay.

Interlude—Legacy

Reshaper Year 1895

Ouran'an, once great city of the Reshapers, was a ruin. A necropolis of hoarfrost spires like the jagged teeth of dragons. A sick, black essence webbed its way along the streets; it crept up buildings like vines. Its gossamer threads extended from the rotted corpses strewn about. It had left none untouched.

Varésh Lúm-talé stood beneath the archway of the city gate and wept, consumed by memories. This was not the first metropolis or people he had failed. He crept inward despairingly—just one more look. A moment in another monument to his failure, this stain of a legacy.

He wrapped his midnight, feathered wings around himself, though it did little to ward away the early morning chill. There was something angry to the cold, something... old. Familiar. Varésh closed his eyes and held his nose to the sky. Being the creature, the abomination that he was, he could discern the various energies in the air—arcane or otherwise—with but a sniff. They were more or less of him, after all.

"Mirkúr." But different than the black essence tattooed to the city and the dead. Less a plague. He opened his eyes and trained them on the tallest spire. Even here, perhaps a mile or two away, he could feel the mirkúr's urgency. He unfurled his wings and, with a great flap, took flight.

MIRKÚR CHOKED THE interior of the spire. Every now and then the energy seemed to hiss, its discontent provoked by the illumination streaming from Varésh's wings. He descended from the topmost balcony, heart thumping, skin like gooseflesh underneath his garb.

There were bodies here, what remained of them at least. The gore had left no ceiling, wall, nor floor untouched. This was where the slaughter had begun, in the halls and chambers of the Reshaperate Spire. Or, at the very least, where the savagery had reached its peak. Varésh pressed on, through the catacombs, and into the depths below.

He touched down in the anteroom; his equilibrium faltered. The world spun in and out of focus momentarily before Varésh was able to steady himself. He took a deep, ragged breath and pressed ahead, crossing overtop the inlay of a black and white raven. Trickster, most believed. Wisdom bringer, Varésh sought to make them see.

Had sought.

The Reshaperate Vaults stood in a hallway wide enough for six to stand abreast. There were nine doors total, the first eight of which stood parallel to one another; the last was further on. Each bore a labyrinth of grooves extending outward from a unique symbol carved in the center of the door. The crests of the eight Reshaperate families. Though they bloomed with light as Varésh passed them by, they remained sealed.

He reached the final door, engraved with the symbol of a raven, wings outstretched. He mimicked the depiction, wispy tendrils of brilliant light—illum—extending from the tips of his wings. The illumination permeated the engraving and the grooves. The door dilated with a groan.

Varésh furled his wings around him like a cloak, light streaming from his feathers to erect a barrier that pushed against the wall of darkness that'd erupted from the vault. Smoke shrieked and crashed against the barricade, forcing

Varésh to expend more illum than he would have liked. The onslaught faltered after a minute or two, leaving silence and a white-eyed silhouette.

Varésh approached at a measured pace. He sensed whatever this creature before him was, it would not hurt him. This was just as well because he'd used up an entire wing's worth of illum.

The silhouette hissed bits and pieces of the old Reshaper tongue, though the words were too distorted to discern.

Varésh shook his head. "I do not understand. I am sorry."

The silhouette swirled and, in a rush of smoke, retreated to the back end of the vault. Varésh followed. The silhouette moaned, and he realized its tether to this plane was growing weak; its form was collapsing. He knelt before it, staring into those white eyes, searching for something, someone—a sign, anything. It mewed again and gestured with a wispy thread of a hand to a grimy leather book.

Varésh picked it up. His heart stopped.

A journal. The journal of a friend, of one whom he'd considered a true son.

The silhouette wailed and, in a burst of mirkúr, ceased to be.

Varésh clutched the leather keepsake to his chest, trembling. He opened the journal and read by the light of his wing. Read until he was numb, and the prospect of death seemed to entice him more than did life. His creations, his *children,* were dead. Some worse than dead, puppets dancing to the tune this tainted mirkúr sang.

He looked at the journal. Where ink related fear and the fall of Ouran'an, it also offered hope, desperate as it was, to quell the plague that entropy had wrought. But for this minuscule chance at reclamation, at redemption, to help see the hope in this journal come to fruition, Varésh was going to have to do the eighteenth most moronic thing he had ever done.

But do I have the strength?

A dead voice, a familiar voice, whispered from the shadow of his mind.

Varésh acknowledged the voice with a tiny nod. As always, it was right.

Journal tucked away, he withdrew from the vaults and the city he had failed.

It was time to swim the Temporal Sea.

Act II

So Much Weight

Dead

Names held power.

Blood was memory.

Dreams were history made manifest.

Avaria blinked. Before him stood a man. Beyond the man, a tree. Beyond the tree, atop a distant hill, the ruin of a city old.

Brightness—soft and warm. Foreign whispers on the wind and a feeling he had seen this all before. Beside him—hounds composed from threads of light. Three hounds, four now five now six—and a seventh near the tree. Seven, then a single beast beside him, the utmost of its kind.

"You've been asleep," the man said. Wings protruded from his back; midnight feathers tapered into mist. Eyes were placid storms. "Do you know me, boy? Do you know me by name?"

Avaria nodded.

"Speak it," said the man. "Speak it now and give me strength."

"Alerion."

Eyes like storm clouds come alive. Illum snaps like lightning in the night. Blood trickling from his eyes. "I have seen this all before."

"Seen what?"

Alerion beckoned with an outstretched hand. "Drink of me and see."

Avaria held his ground. "Show me here."

"I cannot." Alerion advanced. "This place is but a moment in a time long dead and we are naught but ghosts." He stopped short of the snarling hound. "Please—drink of me and *see*."

So Avaria did,

and the meadow

turned

to

ash—but the tree *endured.*

Come, it beckoned with a groaning branch.

Avaria indulged the ancient tree. The sky rained blood; he was alone now in the ruin of this place.

There were trees here once, the lone tree said. *They called me Lost.*

And now? Avaria ran his hand along the gnarled bark.

Memory, said the tree. *Sometimes Sorrow, sometimes Thorn.*

Avaria pressed his forehead to the tree. *And what do you prefer?*

The tree thrummed. *No one... has ever asked me that.* It caressed Avaria with a gentle branch. *Call me... Bringer. Yes, I would like that very much. Bringer...* The name lingered in the bloody air. It held benevolent mystique; it served to ease Avaria's mind as he melded with the tree

and woke with ringing in his ears,

black fire in his chest,

red snow beneath his back.

Find me, Bringer whispered on the wind.

Find her, Alerion whispered in his mind.

"Find *you*..." Avaria uttered to the night,

to the white eyes

gleaming in the gloom.

THERE WAS A warmth to the darkness enfolding the Peaks of Dren. To the cold blanketing Nil-Illúm. Avaria couldn't say what, but it served to his ease his blood, to help him focus on the fact he wasn't dead—not anymore. Not anymore. He was alive. No longer dead—alive like the wisps in the lamps that lit the street. Alive, with breath in his lungs and pain in his heart. Pain—So. Much. Pain.

"Your steps are confident for a man returned from death."

Avaria looked at Erath. "Tell me again—how long?"

"Two months."

"Two months..." Avaria massaged the spot between his eyes. "How...?"

"I was hoping you might tell me," Erath said.

Avaria shrugged. They walked. It snowed. The lamps fell blue from green and the world was silent.

"How did you find me?"

Erath shrugged. "Just... a feeling?" She looked more uncertain than she sounded. She frowned. "Feeling—how are you feeling?"

Three days since she'd found him in the snow.

"Like..." His throat itched with thirst. His mind buzzed like summer flies. Find me. Find her. Find you. "A fragment of a puzzle searching for its kin." Alerion. Blood rain. Bringer—

Hand to his chest. Scar, screaming, pain like needles kissing eyes. Madness grinning in his mind. His mother grinning like the dead—grinning like the dead and laughing like a storm. His mother—dead.

Dead.

Dead.

DEAD.

"She's dead..." he whispered. Felt a hand on his. "My mother."

Dead like all the light in Ulm.

Dead like all the light in Helveden.

Dead.

"We lost a lot that night," said Erath. "Flesh and blood and brick and stone."

"Where is it now—where are *they* now?" Sinhounds. Geph. Avaria ached to rip the beast to bits, tear them all to shreds. Abominations like a fucking cancer in the mouth. Bile at the memory of that grin stretched across his mother's face—Avaria retched. A knot of agony in his head—had she ever really *been*? Retched sour blood. Sickness—this was what it tasted like to be alive. Pungent iron.

"Te Mirkvahíl," Avaria growled.

"Is dead," Erath said.

"Can't be. Sinhounds running wild..."

"Te Mirkvahíl *is dead*," Erath said. "Trust me. This... this is something else."

Avaria processed what she'd said. "What is it?"

"You need to rest," said Erath, but Avaria waved her off.

"*You need*," said a measured voice inside his head, "*to take a breath and grieve. Acting on emotion, on the numbness and the shock, will lead you anywhere but straight.*"

Half-mechanically, Avaria forsook the streets of Nil-Illúm for trees. Trees and weeping shadows, Erath following like a woman dragged along by a crazed longhound on a leash.

"Where"—she yelped, tripping over the log Avaria had leapt; kept her balance—"are you going?"

To scream at dead stars. "To grieve."

Leave him be. Leave him to his misery and his rage.

A flash of light. Spectral baying in his wake.

Erath cursed.

Avaria ran.

SHE STOOD THERE in the glade. The girl of burnt paper flesh and dead moon eyes. Hair like strands of snow and moonlight. Expecting him. Seeking him. Avaria could feel it in his blood, that coldness bonding them. Swaying him, much as it had those months ago in the woods.

"You live." She beckoned with an outstretched hand.

He approached. Stopped. "My mother's dead."

"I know. I can feel it, see it in your memories. I am sorry."

"If you can see my memories—"

"I can see what you experienced in The In Between before you woke," said the girl. "I would ask about Alerion, but your words would be of little help. I would ask about the tree—"

"But my words would be of little help." Avaria narrowed his eyes. "They're familiar to you, aren't they? Bringer and Alerion?" A hint of courage blossomed in his chest. "Am *I* familiar to you? Were we predestined for this meeting, and the last?"

She touched his cheek. Her hand was ice. "Yes."

"Is Te Mirkvahíl dead?"

"Yes."

She was mist and shadow, whispers on the wind.

Gone—as everything he'd known was gone. Desperate questions in the wake of ruin. Who was she? What was she? What was *he*? That knot inside his head—had has mother ever really *been* or had he been the plaything for monstrosities and horror from the start? What was anything—what was the point? What was the point when everything was gone and fucking...

dead.

He fell to his knees. Punched the ground, punched through snow until his hand was numb with cold and maybe pain. Wept a thousand tears of rage and woe, a thousand more for spirits lost, dead and gone. Dead and gone, just like his mother.

Dead.

Gone.

Spell

Time was still. To Erath, at least. Had been for the past two months. So much lost, so many questions raised. She stared into the night sky, at the vast sea of stars, wondering if perhaps they might be the eyes of something monstrous, watching the chaos unfold. Were they naught but playthings?

Two months. No sign of Aveline since they'd gone their separate ways. Avaria Norrith, returned from the dead. Dren, *finally* dead; Erath had seen to that herself. It tugged at her even now, had every day for the past two months. It'd been surprisingly easy to kill him, maybe even a bit... satisfying. What a wretched thought—but what a wretched, twisted thing he'd been. She closed her eyes and breathed deep the chill air, falling into memory.

Wisplit snow and dead trees.

Stillness in the air.

Dren, hands clasped behind his back, dragging limp wings. A ruin rearing up behind him. "You return," he said. "Why?"

"I'm not satisfied with simplicities," Erath said. "You would sacrifice a world to save it, as you said—why? What was so broken about this world that it required saving, *destruction*? I want the truth, Dren. The *entire* truth."

"We are but motes of dust," Dren said. "Grains of sand on a vast beach. Insignificant." He sighed. "I can show you, but you'll not like what you learn. It might even break you."

"I'm already broken," Erath said.

"Aren't we all?" Dren motioned with his hand. "Come."

He led her into the ruin. Deeper yet, to a chamber with the tarnished inlay of a winged trio on the floor. Each was cloaked. Curiosity bloomed in Erath—she had seen these figures before, on the henges in the Wisplands. At the center of the chamber hovered a sphere. Dren touched it with his index finger and a brilliant blue light bloomed within, growing brighter.

"This," he said, "is the Fountainhead, the world from which all others are born." He traced the air; smaller spheres manifested, each connected to the Fountainhead by a strand of light. From those smaller spheres grew orbs of lesser size, tethered to their origins by luminescent threads. "These are the Nexuses and their respective Scions. From the Fountainhead, Nexus worlds; from the Nexuses, Scions—do you understand?"

"A multiverse," said Erath. "You're saying we exist in a multiverse."

Dren nodded.

"But how does any of this relate to temporal alteration?"

"Temporal alteration is the manner by which each new world is created. Every world is a variation of another," Dren said. "You wonder how I could possibly know this..." He closed his eyes. "I have tried many times before—and each time, I have failed. So many names. So many children. So much *death*. My legacy, my child, is destruction, failure."

"You still haven't answered my question," Erath said. "What was so broken about this world that it required your definition of saving?"

Dren opened his eyes. "Not just this world—*all* worlds. I thought if I could return to the Fountainhead—no... travel *beyond* the Fountainhead—I might be able to prevent any of this from ever happening. Fold the worlds, as it were, by quelling madness."

Erath glanced at the inlay, then back at Dren. "Does it have anything to do with them? Those figures?"

"Everything," Dren uttered. He waved his hand and, to Erath's horror and disgust, manifested The Raven's Rage. "I was a fool, my child. I cannot be trusted; I am weak." He waved his hand again and the blade shattered, leaving a silhouette of energy. "She will come for me. Come for *this*. The blade itself is useless—it's the energy she wants. Take it."

Erath took a step back. "Who is *she*? I... why give this to me?" What did Dren expect *her* to do with... with whatever power this was? "I'm nothing. I'm useless."

Dren waved his hand a third time and the energy—*energies*—wreathed Erath, embraced her. "You, dear child, are *not* useless. You are everything. This will help you see. Take it. Kill me. Flee."

The memory fizzled; Erath found herself looking up at the stars. Two months and she still hadn't a clue what anything meant. Hadn't an inkling as to how to use the energies Dren had gifted her, let alone who "She" was.

Tickle in her ear. Stupid buzzing. Smacked at the phantom bug thing, whatever it was. More buzzing. Whispers. She was going mad, fuck it all. Made sense. World had gone to shit—why shouldn't she?

"Help."

Erath started. She'd heard that clearly, hadn't she? A voice asking for help. She looked about. Snow, trees, darkness. Not a soul to be seen.

"Help... me."

Okay. She had *definitely* heard that. In her head? Somewhere nearby? A shift in the atmosphere, a twinkle, a fold of light. She grasped at it, catching only air. Another blink—southward. She followed. Through a frosted copse to a clearing and an overlook below which stretched a meadow vast. For a moment Erath wondered what it might be like to walk the grass, to feel the sunlight kiss her flesh. So many years... She could scarcely recall the sensation.

"Help."

The voice snapped her from her trance. It had grown louder without a doubt, but still there was nothing and no one to whom the phantom voice belonged. She frowned, eyes narrowed, and swiped at the air with her index finger. A twist of light, a throng of screams, gone as quickly as they'd come. Erath stood motionless, mouth agape, adrenaline rushing through her like a spring stream. Again—more screams, distant, disembodied, indiscernible cries. What in the Raven's name had she stumbled across? Erath had long lost her ability to wield illum—what was this?

"Dren," she whispered. Those energies with which he'd wreathed her... She traced the air a third time, forming the letter S. Myriad pictures snapped across her mind, too quickly for Erath to make any sense of what she saw. Maybe there was a method to all this madness. Seeing things, hearing distant voices—had she tore through the seams which kept the worlds apart? A crazy thought, and yet...

"Show me, uh..." Gods, what did she want to see? "Spring. A century and a half ago." She traced the letter S once more— and rivulets of color dripped from the sky, as if to erase the present and manifest the past. Gone was night, were snow and darkness; here bloomed blades of green and rainbow flowers. A blue sky and sunlight. Erath looked at her hands— they retained their paleness, but the world around her was so much more. She stared, wide-eyed, body tingling, warmth blooming in her chest, just atop her heart. She'd all but forgotten what *this* looked like.

And then it was gone, in a flash of light, and motes of luminescence scattered to the wind, leaving Erath alone with the snow and the stars and her thoughts. If only Aveline were here. Maybe she'd have an idea of what any of this was. Fuck it all, if only Dren had *told her what it was...* Miserable winged bastard. She chewed her lip. There *was* one other she might ask, and he was the wisest man Erath knew, had ever known.

ALMOST THREE MONTHS since Leru's death. How slow time seemed to have moved since then. Agonizing. Cold. Like Fenrin's memories. Leru, spirit dwelling somewhere with her sister, Alor. Fenrin heaved a sigh to the lamplit streets; he walked them every night in thought, had for years, so many he'd lost count. Shortly before Alor's death. Murder. He thought of his daughters in their infancy, of the days they were born, and longed for the innocence of such moments. The world was a dark place. Sad. Sorry. Fenrin was the utmost of his kind in this regard, walking cloaked in darkness, in the knowledge he and he alone had been untouched by the Burn. Unsullied while his people were confined to rock and snow and shadow. What a wretched life.

Nil-Illúm was still and silent save his footsteps and his clouded breath. Save the occasional rustling of leaves or the crowing of night fowl. Eerie, that. The world. On edge these last two months since Helveden's fall. Sinhounds. Fenrin shook his head; they'd left none alive. A city so large, yet not a soul had survived.

Unless, he thought, *one counts the prince.* Strange prince. Prince of Misery he was known as here in Nil-Illúm. Lord of Sorrow, Prince of Woe, the list went on and on. Not a slight, but sympathy. Fenrin knew his story well—a babe discovered in the snow, kept and cared for by the late queen as her own. Another sigh, and a prayer for the many dead from the realm from which his daughter's murderers had come. Perhaps this was penance, not that Fenrin would have wished such atrocities upon the city and her people. They were not responsible for Alor's death; that had been a select few—and *they* had paid dearly. For a half second, Fenrin thirsted for blood, but the craving passed as quickly as it had come; he was not that man, that monster anymore.

But maybe I ought to be. Things were mad. Maybe monsters were necessary. Maybe only monsters could fight monsters. What was the old saying? From chaos, law. Dren had taught him that; Dren was dead, had gone mad ages ago. Fenrin had seen his memories prior to his death. Temporal alteration.

Elseworlds. Fascinating. Horrific, even. Fascinating, none-theless. He should like to see them. Maybe they held the key to... to what? Rectification? Reclamation? All of that, temporal alteration, the price... seemed far too high, far too risky. And yet... *From chaos, law.* Gods knew this was a lawless world, growing less by the day.

He was in the courtyard, now, of his home, a mountain manor. At the center stood those triptych effigies, winged and cloaked. They had been here since before Fenrin and his peo-ple had come to be, so said Dren. Creators. He took the walk-way with measured steps, breathing the chill air. Shadowed footsteps, though, drew his eyes, and from the trees to his left came a rather frazzled looking woman.

Fenrin cocked an eyebrow. "Never one for the straightfor-ward path, my girl."

"I... Something—spell," said Erath hastily. "I did *some-thing*. Saw, heard things." She doubled over, catching her breath, then rose to meet his eyes. "Has to do with Dren."

Fenrin narrowed his eyes. "What of him?"

Erath looked frantically about. "I... I think I'm *seeing* his memories and..." She looked at Fenrin unblinkingly, such fear in those stark white eyes. "It has to do with The Raven's

Rage."

THEY SAT IN Fenrin's study, Erath in a chair by the window, Fenrin at his desk. Silence reigned, had for some minutes as Fenrin went through everything that Erath had relayed about Dren, The Raven's Rage, the Burn, and this newfound ability of hers. Truthfully, it was a lot to take in, but Fenrin had time. Gods knew he had *so much time.*

"I'm not mad," he said. "If you were worried. Not at you, at least." He sighed. "I suppose I shouldn't be surprised about Dren, yet I am... and am not at the same time, if that makes any sense." Erath nodded. "First things first—*you* now wield the power, the energies that resided in The Raven's Rage."

Again, Erath nodded. "But I don't know what it is."

"Radich, I would venture," Fenrin said. "Possibility. The power wielded by the person Dren was *before* he was Dren. This Varésh Lúm-Talé, whomever he was. *What*ever he was."

"Do you think I'm seeing his memories?" Erath asked. "Hearing them?"

"With radich, anything is possible," said Fenrin. "Or so I understand. As I have never wielded the energy, I cannot say for certain." He frowned. "Did he mention anything more of this *She*?"

Erath shook her head. "He seemed afraid of whatever *She* was, *is*. Said he couldn't be trusted, so he bestowed"—she gestured wildly—"upon me, the lot of good that's going to do. I have no idea what I'm doing. I haven't for ages."

"If it makes you feel better," Fenrin said, "neither do I. I simply take things one day at a time." There was a twinkle in her eyes. Something on the tip of her tongue. "Ask your question."

"I'm afraid it might be rude," Erath said, averting his gaze.

Fenrin stood and approached. He knelt before her, hands on her shoulders, and looked her in the eyes. "Whatever the question, it's important. Please, Erath—ask me."

She heaved a ragged sigh. "You were untouched by the Burn, yet you dwell in the darkness of the Peaks as do the rest of the drenarians. Why? Why not be free?"

He caressed her cheek. "There is no freedom for me when the rest of my people are in chains. I am not free until we *all* are free, however long that may take. I'm not going anywhere, Erath."

She closed her eyes a moment, swallowing; he could tell she'd forced back tears. She opened her eyes. "What do I do?

What do *we* do? Sinhounds and this thing, this *She* running amok. This power of mine, if you can even call it that. *What* is happening?"

"I'm not sure," Fenrin said. An honest answer. "We might start with the prince you rescued from the snow. Dead, now quite alive—not a feat attainable by many."

"He's lost so much," Erath said. "His mother."

"Ahnil Norrith was a noble woman," Fenrin said. "Her passing pains me, as does Helveden's ruin. It disturbs me too. Sinhounds not bound to the will of Te Mirkvahíl—to what, then?"

"As you said, my king," Erath said. "We might start with the prince."

Parable

Day. Night. In the Peaks it was all the same; the persistent darkness made it impossible to tell, made it feel like time had all but slowed. So much on his mind. His mother. Virtuoso Khal. Norema. Helveden. Even strange Nameless Head, whom Avaria presumed dead. Never had gotten his name, never had gotten his story. Had he found what he was looking for in Rach Na'Schuul? Hard to say as Avaria had been dead the entire time.

His thoughts shifted to—could he even call it a dream? Whatever it was he'd experienced before waking in the snow. Alerion. Bringer. Find Bringer. Find a woman. Find himself. Seemed clear as day yet muddled all the same. He wished Geph was here, first so he could ring the bastard's neck, maybe gouge his eyes out based on what he'd seen, then to have him help Avaria make sense of all this shit. Geph had always been good at that, interpreting dreams.

"What happened, Geph?" Avaria murmured to the trees. Walking helped; he got antsy if he sat still for too long. "What I saw... was that really you?" Could have been; there was a lot Avaria didn't know about the longhound—sinhound?—and it made him wonder what secrets Geph might have been keeping. Had his kind been something more at one point? Gods, but his chest ached. *Everything* ached, outward, inward to the depths of his being. Felt like vines constricting his heart, vines with knives that liked to twist in wounds.

Mother's grin.

Norema's corpse.

He started, leaned against a tree, feeling winded, exhausted.

Any of you, he thought wearily. To his sinhounds or whatever thing now lurked within. *Please. Just...* He heaved a ragged sigh, on the cusp of sobbing for the second time in what, an hour or two? How the hell was any of this real? Was this what it had been like as a babe, alone in the snow and trees? Was this what utter helplessness felt like? Cold and hollow. Dark. Avaria closed his eyes—where had he come from? The thought had grazed his mind a few times over the years, but only now did it linger, festering like an open wound, *begging* for attention. Where. What. Why. Where had he come from? What was he? Why was he here? Surely the universe would see fit to answer these questions after subjecting him to such a torturous life, a hellish fuck-knew-how-many weeks since he'd departed Helveden looking for that sword. He clung to the tree as the tears came, as sobs racked his body.

"Mama..."

But that safety was gone. Dead, lingering only as a maddened grin stretched wide across his mind. Haunting every step he took and everything he dreamt.

"You know what you must do," said a voice. Commanding, soft. Avaria looked around, realized it was in his head. *"Stand up, Avaria Norrith. Stand up, Prince of Ariath. It would pain your mother to see you so."*

He pushed himself to stand straight, tall; wiped his tears away with his arm. *You spoke to me the other day,* he said. *I saw you in my dream, whatever it was. You were beside me as I faced Alerion.* A hound of light. *What are you? By what name do I call you?*

"I am Jor, the allhound," it said, *"and when last we truly spoke you were but a boy. Much has changed since then; dying has a way of, shall we say, resetting things. In dying, in rebirth, you freed me,*

made the seven whole."

Sins. Seven sins, you mean, Avaria said. *The worst of me.*

"No," said Jor. "*It is not so black and white as that. Sin*—true *sin*—*is not indicative of evil, nor is it a representation of your worst self, just as true honor is not indicative of good intent. Sinhounds and honorhounds are merely two sides of the same coin.*"

What are allhounds?

"We are the balance," Jor said. "*The middle ground.*"

I see, Avaria said, trying to comprehend it all. *What more of me do you know?*

"Nothing you don't already know yourself," Jor said. "What mysteries remain, we shall uncover together in due time—and I think you know where all roads lead."

Banerowos, Avaria uttered. *Dead city of a dead race. So many times, I saw it, walked it in my dreams. Never thought that it was real. Not until...* Images flashed across his mind. The tower. The descent. Alerésh. Schisms in continuity. A city vast and bright; a city dead, snow-draped ruin and a symphony of shrieks. *The answers are all there.* He could feel it in his bones, in the tingling of his heart. The howling of his mind, something buried yearning to break free.

"Her," he murmured. That girl of burnt paper flesh. He

suddenly yearned for her presence, that connection. Everything had been predestined. "Luminíl." The name came to his lips, escaped his tongue of its own volition. Her name was Luminíl. To the darkness and the cold, he whispered, "Find me."

Then, he sat and waited.

LUMINÍL HAD SEEN no further than this moment. Everything from here on out was fate's design. She found the Prince of Woe, as the drenarians had taken to calling him, in a copse, leaning back against a tree. He met her with an unblinking stare.

"You told me my words would be of little use to you," he said, standing to his full height. "But you, Luminíl—yes, I know your name—have words that would be of great use to me. I can feel it." He tapped his skull. "You claim to have seen what I experienced in The In Between—but did you see *everything*? My escape through the labyrinth of my mind? A girl in the forest 'neath a tree—"

"What girl?" Luminíl asked. "What tree?" Trees. So many trees.

"Beneath a tree of corpses strung to dance the dance of

death," Avaria said. "Garbed in black. Eyes like the abyss. Like you—but *not* you." He paced. Muttered to himself. "... Dreams and memories braid together with those belonging to a monster." Looked at Luminíl. "Never saw that tree, never saw that forest around Banerowos in my life, in my dreams. I felt her fear as if it were my own. She—whatever *she* is—possessed my corpse in Rach Na'Schuul. I need answers."

"She calls herself Hush," said Luminíl. "And I loved her once. She will not stop, and I cannot rest until she is stopped— but she is strong. Desperate. And desperate people do monstrous things." She averted Avaria's gaze. "So much horror..."

If you had not left her...

If you had helped her, not tormented her...

Gods. Was Luminíl to blame? Had she driven Hush mad all those millennia ago atop the ruins of Banerowos? *No*, she thought. *Hush was mad long before that.* But maybe Luminíl had been the straw that broke the camel's back. Maybe she had snapped Hush beyond rectification.

"What does she want?" Avaria asked.

"Me," Luminíl said. "Reclamation. We are all of us prey to the world maker parable. This"—she held her arms out wide—"was wrought by Hush, Alerion, and myself, and damn it all if we three are not monsters."

She expected shock of a sort from Avaria, yet he remained calm; something in him had changed. *He* had changed consistently over the months; Luminíl yearned to know why. He was more than he seemed.

"Power corrupts. A small taste is toxic, seductive. Especially destructive when wielded by liars," she said. "Hush betrayed me, tainted me; as long as she roams, as long as she is awake, so too am I."

"You seem exhausted," Avaria said. "And I'm not just saying that."

"You are different," Luminíl said. "Grieving yet composed. What changed?"

"I died," Avaria said, "and it released my allhound. Restored internal balance."

Allhounds were rare, especially now, though their numbers once had been great. That was millennia ago, however, during the time of the Reshapers. Luminíl had interacted with them scarcely, but their center, their equilibrium, was renowned.

"You will need that balance if you are to confront Hush," Luminíl said. "If *we* are to confront her. She is mad; whatever means to reclamation she seeks is sure to be desperate, destructive."

"Temporal alteration," Avaria said. "Only thing that would make sense."

Luminíl nodded. "Decidedly desperate and destructive, especially if the whispers are true." Avaria tilted his head. "Elseworlds. A multiverse as some would say. New realities wrought through changes to the past."

Avaria furrowed his brow, tense his jaw. "...Might explain things. Alerésh, Varésh, Alerion, and another—different, yet so similar." He looked at Luminíl. "If what you say is true then... might they all be one and the same?"

Luminíl sneered at the mention of Varésh. "In a manner of speaking. What you must understand is Varésh and Alerion are—*were* two very different people. As I said, power is seductive, corruptive; Varésh murdered Alerion and wore him as a guise. Alerésh is nothing more than a sorry abomination— and very much dead. I found his corpse in Rach Na'Schuul."

Silence. Calm snow. Avaria's chest rose and fell slowly as he contemplated what she had said. He was so very different, almost unnervingly so. "What happens now?" he asked.

"We seek Hush," said Luminíl, "and put a stop to her madness lest she break the world." Footsteps. She spun about—the drenarian king and a young drenarian woman. Familiar... Luminíl breathed deeply, narrowed her eyes. Familiar and wielding something great, wild. Dangerous.

They stopped short of Luminíl. The king regarded her with bright silver eyes; he kneeled, motioning for the young woman to do so as well. They bowed their heads. "Great Luminíl," he said. "We are humbled by your presence."

Gods but it had been *ages* since someone had referred to her as such. Honorifics were... Well. Used far too liberally in reference to far too many monstrous people. But him, this drenarian—king was befitting.

"Rise," Luminíl said. "Your respect is admirable, but you need not refer to me as such." She cocked her head. How had he known her—

Dren. Of course. She eyed this king. More than what he seemed.

"I am Fenrin," he said, he and his companion rising. "And this is Erath." He met Avaria's eyes. "I am glad to see you well, all things considered." Did not wait for a response; looked from Avaria to Luminíl and back. "There are matters I would discuss in the safety of Nil-Illúm."

There were ears everywhere. Wicked eyes. The trees watched silently. Hush was mistress of the night, of shadows, shade, and silhouette—she would learn of things eventually. As such, Luminíl cared little where they spoke. She gave a small nod.

"As you wish."

JUDGING BY AVARIA'S yawn, it was late when they had caught each other up on everything. Allhounds. Radich. The potential for Erath to see Dren's memories, to bend time recollectively. Hush. The many lies of Varésh Lúm-talé. What a mess. What an absolute, chaotic mess. Not that he was surprised. Everything was out of sorts, had been for a while, so why not make it even fucking crazier?

"Breathe," Jor said in Avaria's mind.

Trying.

"I learned a saying," Jor said. *"Remembered, rather, and I think it pertinent to the situation, to the world at large—from chaos, law. Do you understand?"*

Familiar words, though Avaria swore he had never heard such an aphorism. *From madness comes order, or something along those lines,* he thought. *But how strong a hold must pandemoni-*

um have before it finally relents, before the balance shifts and peace prevails?

"In this case? Quite strong," Jor said. *"This thing, this Hush..."* He trailed off. *"She is entropy. Desperation. She is* the source— the mother *of mirkúr."* Luminíl had been clear as day about that. Hush—the Vulture. The thought made him cold. Memories flashed; darkness in a dead wood. She had scraped his mind; in doing so, however, she had let him into hers. New bits and pieces had arisen in the last several hours.

"All roads, it seems, lead to Banerowos," said Fenrin after a time. So much silence. Pensive. "What remains of it at least." He acknowledged them all unblinkingly. "The way is long—I have been there once myself." Drew a look from Erath. "As the sunlight stings my kind, I propose an alternative route— Underlight."

What the fuck was Underlight?

"Through Gil'an Mor, City of Hounds," Luminíl murmured. She sounded less than thrilled. "Dead city of a dying race. Dangerous. Hush is the mother of sinhounds."

Geph. Sinhound? How? So many questions. Bastard hound. Was he alive? Hounds. Strange beasts. Existed internally and externally—how? So. Many. Questions. Maybe

Gil'an Mor would lead to Geph; maybe he could save Geph or... something. Avaria rubbed the spot between his eyes and sighed.

"Chaos squeezes tighter yet," said Jor.

No shit. Know anything of Gil'an Mor?

"Dangerous. Old."

How informative.

"You said we seek Hush," Avaria said to Luminíl. "But the way it sounds? We're luring her—to the genesis and the end. The genesis *of* her end." Poetic, that. Sad. What a sad thing Hush was. What sad things they *all* were, immortals and mortals alike.

"I imprisoned her there once," Luminíl said. "I will do so again—permanently." Permanence was a scary thing, especially, as Avaria had come to learn, it meant jack shit when things saw fit to resurrect. Luminíl looked at Erath. "You are the key—your radich."

Erath swallowed. "That's reassuring." She yawned; Avaria yawned.

"For now, though, sleep," said Luminíl. "The journey ahead is long."

"You mean for us to leave tomorrow?" Avaria asked, and

Luminíl gave a brief nod. "Right then. Sleep."

BLINK.

Ouran was, and the world was. He stood in tall grass, gold beneath the sun; a crisp breeze swayed the feathers of his wings. In the distance he saw snowcapped mountains, and the shadow of a memory said that that was where he had to go.

He stretched his wings, sore with the ache of sleep; he could tell that they had not been used for some time. The breeze knocked his hood back; the cool air against his face was refreshing and it made his beak tingle—the sky called to him. He tried to flap his wings but could not, so he walked.

And walked.

The world was placid. Thick wispy threads of light flittered through the air and he watched them, cocked his head as they descended toward him. They had eyes and mouths, their bodies were translucent and encasing orbs of light.

Memory pulsed. They were Indrisori eels, carriers of light—the sheep to his people's shepherds.

Another pulse: where were his people—who were his people? Ouran waited for a third throb to present the answers, but none came. Perhaps they would later.

He saw trees on his journey toward the mountains. Their flowers bloomed like white stars and the eels followed him like hungry cats, expecting him to lead them to a bowl of warm milk. He ran a gentle talon through his feathers, subduing an itch above his eyes, only for it to retreat down to his wings.

Fly. He strained to flap.

Fly. His great wings twitched.

Fly. With one massive buffet he ascended.

And ascended further yet.

This place, this world... it looked so different from this height, like a painting or a pastel piece on paper. The landscape swayed and swirled beneath the breeze and Ouran shot forward with another beat of his wings, the Indrisori eels at his heels.

The plains below gave way to copses small and large; then to a lake, still as death; and finally, plains again, these littered sporadically with trees. Ouran thought of his people again; he thought of people in general, and of fauna. Where had they all gone off to—why was this beautiful place so still?

Ouran flew straight for hours. At dusk he descended into

a valley that spoke of ages long passed. Buried underneath the grass and dried out weeds he saw the rusted remnants of train tracks. Trains, memory reminded him, had not been used for thousands of years, since the last of the humans had gone extinct.

He saw the carcasses of great locomotives, some electric, others undoubtedly steam. This place was a graveyard, a wasteland for the old and unnecessary things of the world. There were automobiles and airplanes too. Maybe, he thought, this place had once been a museum of sorts; he could make out the faint remnants of a structural base.

Much later he settled in for the night against the base of a tree. The eels revolved around him as if he were a planet. His wings were drawn about him like a cloak; his hood was pulled past his eyes. Stars blinked, and he watched a volley race across the sky.

Ouran closed his eyes to the night and dreamt of snow, of stars reflecting in the snow, of beams of light ascending from the earth and rocks.

And darkness.

TWILIGHT.

A series of cerebral pulses shook Ouran from sleep, and for a while he stared at the distant peaks that he must reach. They were called Phantaxis: The Door to Heaven, the Indrisori lands. "Come and know," they whispered on the breeze. This far out he could smell the snow and rock. They were memories, but of what?

Another pulse informed him he had sought Phantaxis before. A second and third—these painful, like his skull was being squeezed—told him that his people, the Indrisori, the Celestials, were there and awaiting his arrival. They had to be, for their time on Indris was coming to its end.

Thunder shook the cloudless sky; the tree trunk buzzed against his back. Instinctively Ouran started to his feet and took to the wind. He rode the current north amidst the booms and intermittent burst of stars, the eels mewing at the bedlam. They snaked around his arms, quivering, their light flickering. Ouran picked up speed, and the faster he went the less the eels' light became, until they were translucent, slumbering shells.

At dawn he touched down in the gray corpse of a once proud city.

Pulse.

His city.

He walked at a measured pace, wings half-cocked. The breeze of the world remained here too, slipping through old windows and doorways, through cracks and crevices—a dirge of days long past, a specter.

Clank.

He froze.

Clank. Clink.

He looked about, talons splayed.

The sounds came again, louder, closer, more.

Ouran ascended with a flap and took perch on the edge of a ruined tower. A couple hundred feet below the sounders manifested, dragging rusted limbs around street corners and over debris. They bore his image, rusted, wings mangled, twisting all directions. Their heads groaned as they scanned for Ouran, so he assumed, and shrieks like metal scraping metal slipped between their beaks.

"Let our earthen children cleanse the damned," said a voice in the center of his mind. Images flashed: forges and foundries, figures of great height; threads of light erupting from the tips of silver swords, ricocheting off tower shields of glass. A rebellion. The figures in the pictures screeched and

Ouran tottered from his perch, dazed by their refrain. His wings went numb; it was a hand of trembling talons gripping the perch that kept him from plummeting to the street. He shook away the strange fatigue and hoisted himself up and in to sit on a ledge, back to the wall, cloaked by his wings.

His eyes fell shut, and once again Ouran dreamed of the mountains Phantaxis and his people awaiting his arrival. He was their king, and he must be the one to first set foot into Heaven, the Indrisori realm. He saw beams of blue, wreathed in a flurry of snow; beyond them a window into green pastures; in those pastures stood and beckoned figures wrought from wind—no! They were the creators of the wind.

Stars. Snow.

Ouran blinked the dreams away, greeted by the white dusk and the mountain breeze. His feathers were frosted, and icicles hung from the tip of his beak. He snapped them off and pushed himself to his feet, wings spread. The eels, still coiled around his arms, had regrown a morsel of their light, it like the wool of the sheep of old, infinite.

"Come and know." The wind's words were taunting now. "Come and see."

Ouran flapped and fled this place, this city of dead metal

and ruin. Through the trees he went, to the mountain's base, and up its face. A cry escaped his beak, like a dragon woke from sleep. Gray and white was all he saw as he ascended, and soon just white, the cold chaos of the world engulfing him as memory surged and nearly shook him from the sky.

He landed on a small cliff, drawing on the eels' light, what they could offer at least, to steady his mind. More constructs, more technology; Indrisori brand he now knew. He saw his people struck down by their fabricated twins, turned to ash by light, carved for supper by swords.

Ouran pushed himself to complete the ascent, to reach the highest peak, which he found was not incredibly high so much as it was a gradual northward incline. He touched down on the snowcapped rock and hurried toward the cave mouth yards away. It yawned like a leviathan, wide enough to fit perhaps one hundred figures abreast.

Silence greeted him inside and he was reminded momentarily of the stillness he had found in the plains. It was done away by a violent tremor and a loud atmospheric crack. Behind him stars crashed against Phantaxis—the end was near.

Again, he hurried, coming to the center of this barren cave in minutes. An archway reared before him, seven hovering diamonds of varying size, and before it a console of sorts—a lightway marker. And his people were not here. Ouran clucked, perturbed.

"Again, the Eel Lord enters lightless," hissed the cave, hissed something in the cave. "Like so many times before, and forever shall it be."

Light javelined toward him from the shadows. Shock kept him from crying out as his wings fell clean away; the brilliance had cauterized the stumps. He leapt to one side as the burst came again, the hiss fluctuating, now a sonorous cackle.

The assailant leapt from hiding, a monstrous metal-flesh amalgamation—a cyborg, it would have been called centuries ago. It swung its great blade in arches, choreographing the light, making the destructive essence dance before it wound toward Ouran and caught him square in the chest.

Images came hazy as he writhed, grew fuller as the writhing turned to spasms.

"When you attempt to play god, Eel Lord, sometimes you create monsters."

The amalgam vaulted toward him. It froze halfway and sputtered, leaking something black and foul. And then it crumbled to the floor, one eye blinking erratically. "I-I—Indris-ori-ori—i-Ind—risori haaaiiiillll..."

It powered down, dead by the unknown.

No, Ouran realized, discerning a thin barrier between them, projected weakly by the eels around his arms. They mewed, their light pulsating—it was his key away from this beautiful, awful world he had called home.

He stood, groaning, feathers hissing with snuffed smoke. The lightway marker blinked, ready to accept the eels' light as payment for an egress. Ouran held his arms above the orb and the light streamed forth, and the archway shimmered with a picture of the Indrisori land beyond.

Ouran stepped toward it, into it, and through it—but he had not gone anywhere.

And he shrieked like a creature butchered in the night as the memories came in full, a tidal wave of chaos. Light snapped, his people screamed, his people turned to wispy motes of luminescence and ascended through the archway as the Indrisori chained him to this place so long ago.

"Those who are not gods, those who are not judges, should not attempt to be what they are not," the Indrisori snarled in his mind.

Ouran saw—he saw himself, sword in hand, blue light

cutting down his people under proclamations of impurity. So many turned to ash.

To ash.

To ash.

Ash.

Ash.

Ash

Ash.

Ash.

He sputtered. From the center of his chest emerged a blade, and he heard that horrible metal-flesh whisper in his ear as darkness took him from Phantaxis.

BLINK.

Ouran was, and the world was. He stood in tall grass, gold beneath the sun; a crisp breeze swayed the feathers of his wings. In the distance he saw snowcapped mountains, and the shadow of a memory said that that was where he had to go.

Monsters

Indris was but a distant memory in a dream. Likely dead and gone, as were so many of the things and people Varésh Lúm-talé had known. Destruction was a cruel legacy, unforgiving and relentless. He breathed deeply the air of this place, this underdark, this underlight—*the* Underlight as it was known, as the dead halls whispered. What a wretched place in which to have emerged. Alas, to swim the Temporal Sea was to invite chance. So be it.

Varésh winced, snarled at a snap in the center of his mind. He'd been afraid of that—the Varésh Lúm-talé of this reality yet remained; he would have to take a different name lest the consequence of paradox erode his cognizance and turn him into something rambling and mad. Such was the rule by which the Elseworlds were governed.

Ouran, he thought at the pain, this sentient, phantom reaper of identities. For all his power there was still much

Varésh—no, *Ouran*—did not understand about temporal al-teration and the Elseworlds, about the consequence of para-dox—mainly the reason for its existence. Why should anyone care about myriad iterations of an individual running amok? Why should the universe give a shit?

"Because," said the voice in his head, *"such a thing breeds chaos."*

There is much that does, Ouran thought. *Why should it mat-ter?*

"Still ignorant after all of these years," the voice chided. It called itself Alerion; its very existence made Ouran sick for it reminded him of who he had been, was, and always would be. *"Have you learned nothing from the illum network, nothing of and from the Elseworlds?"*

I have learned plenty, Ouran thought.

"Then you would understand the consequence of paradox is only relevant should you encounter the Varésh Lúm-talé of this re-ality," Alerion said. He paused. *"Oh—I see. You* are *aware; you simply choose to wear your given name, your* true name *as opposed to running further."*

The guilt will always call you back, Ouran thought. *Best em-brace my sins and seek redemption. Penance, even.* Gods knew he'd done horrible things. Atrocities. Genocide. What a monster. *Maybe this undertaking is my penance...* He shook his head. Hell was certainly a place of one's own making.

Ouran walked the darkness at a measured pace, wings furled like a cloak. Dim light emanated from his feathers; strange pastel illumination bled from wispy strands of... something. Ouran reached for one, felt cold and fear as the gossamer thing brushed his hand; shattered memories shrieked across his mind.

"Memories," he murmured. His stomach dropped. "*Souls.*" Gods—what had happened here? He sniffed the old air but discerned nothing he was not already familiar with—illum and mirkúr. Even still, their presence here concerned him.

Do you think it was her? he asked Alerion. *Mirkvahíl?*

"*Her or Luminíl,*" Alerion said. "*No telling which. The journal was not clear.*"

It all feels horribly repetitive, Ouran thought. *Seeking the Phoenix and the Vulture.* Hell was history rounding the corner to repeat itself. *A place of my own making.* He shuddered to think of what this reality was like, hoped it wasn't too far gone. Gods knew the Elseworlds were a whirl of entropy and law, locked in a constant tug of war; many realities had fallen prey to desolation.

Did this place exist whence we came? Ouran asked.

"In one way or another, yes," Alerion said. As with everything, there was much about Alerion that Ouran had yet to comprehend despite their millennia of coexistence. *"Everything is a reflection of itself."*

Darkness, cold, and hush. Quietus. A labyrinth of a tomb—a tomb of memory. Ouran longed to be free of the despondency, to smell fresh air and taste the open sky—but instinct kept him here beneath the light, drove him deeper into silent madness. *A sign. Anything—point me in the right direction.*

Whatever that was.

TE MIRKVAHÍL HAS proven to be far more of a problem than Hush had anticipated. When she slew her by the stream, Hush did not foresee the three-month coma and confinement in a labyrinthine mind that would follow. As she ascends the Peaks of Dren she feels... strangely whole—but why? She ruminates a moment, but the answer keeps concealed. Nothing she saw, experienced in three months of sleep sticks out unless one counts the various mental blocks now guarding Te Mirkvahíl's most precious thoughts.

You will tell me all you know, she thinks of the stolen flesh she wears. *They always do.*

A child sprawled atop the rocks. Blanketed in snow. Breathing. Faint yet resolute. In the distance, Ouran'an—the corpse of it at least.

The memory fades. Hush feels pain in her chest, in the depths of her heart—this momentary recollection is hers. But what is the significance? Who is the child? What brought her so near Ouran'an—and when?

"Time and memory are such troubling things," an inner voice opines. This thing too is familiar; Hush is no stranger to voices in her head.

Which one are you? So many—too many to keep track of.

"The worst one." Such certainty. It fails to give a name—a silent challenge.

And where have you been all this time?

"Here. Caged in the abyss. Waiting..."

Waiting. For how long, Hush wonders, and for what?

"You were always a fan of puzzles—you have plenty of pieces to put into place."

Another challenge. So many questions.

"Keep it together, now." Or else.

Silence. Cold air on stolen flesh. An ache in the center of her mind. The difficulty of this undertaking has increased—and that is saying quite a lot as temporal alteration on the scale that Hush envisions is by no means guaranteed. The re-iteration of this fact sends shivers up her spine; the notion of a life sans Luminíl brings tears to Hush's eyes, forms a lump in her throat.

Walk. Do not think. Just walk.

The shadows whisper of a temporal rift. Small, but significant, nonetheless.

A name rides the darkened mountain wind.

Hush smiles.

DREAMS ARE FILLED with beauty. To Hush, that is what defines them—the absolute surrealness of a pale sky and the warmth of her beloved's hand. But Hush cannot recall when last she had a dream, for her thoughts and reveries are monstrous things. Labyrinthine phantasmagorias at the end of which her lovely Luminíl fades to ash. To smoke. To nothingness. Her nightmares are such that she cannot recall, exactly, how things fell apart.

The voice inside her head laughs. *"Mother Sin. What a*

name. The irony…"

Hush knows of what it speaks, of the atrocity so profound she buried it within the darkest corner of her mind. Suppressed it. Feared it—*still* fears it. She shudders, not from the chill of the Peaks or the ever-present darkness nipping at her cheeks, but from the knowledge of a lesson she learned long ago: the guilt will always call you back. And oh, how guilty a thing Hush is. She does not need to know, to remember what she did to taste the lingering iniquity, to feel that harsh, violent tugging at the center of her chest that pulls her toward the past—to the corpse of Banerowos bordered by the Hang-Dead Forest and its myriad restless souls.

"I will fix this," she murmurs—to herself, to Luminíl, and to the world.

Hush does not want to be a monster.

But she is.

Her thoughts drift, drawn to the memory of the boy and the rocks and the snow and the distant ruin of the city Ouran'an. It tugs at her, whispers—but what is the significance? Who is the boy? Hush clenches her hand into a fist, hard enough that her fingernails pierce the flesh of her palm. No blood. Just… something. Whatever it is that sustains her. Smoke and fluid smelling of old rain and rot. A twist of mirkúr.

"Tell me," she whispers. "Please."

The memory fades—now is not the time.

Hush walks.

And walks.

And.

Walks.

GEPH THOUGHT OF his mother and wept as he crossed the old meadow. This horrible place seemed to exhume the sorriest of things, of memories and dreams. Seemed to amplify the guilt and longing and despair. What would she think could she see him now? Sinhound. Murderer. Betrayer. Weakling. To have been so easily swayed by Hush...

But she promised—so much had she promised. Where was she, then? Three months—three months and not a sound, memory, nor scent. Nothing to betray her whereabouts. Did she yet endure?

The question nagged at Geph, for he had headed south of his own volition. Compelled by curiosity, spellbound by the history of Hush; she had, for but a single moment, given him a glimpse inside her mind. Wondrous. Horrifying. Not of his own accord, then. Rather, of and of not. Perhaps it was his very nature—drawn to madness, monstrousness, and misery—that pushed him onward toward a place called Hang-Dead Forest. A cursed barrier behind which sat the corpse of Banerowos. The first great city to arise; the first to fall. Hush's home.

"Always were a curious one, Gephorax," said the voice that'd come to him the night of Helveden's fall. Nameless even now. *"Do you think it wise, your destination, or does something deeper drive you on? Someone, perhaps?"*

Would that he could, said Geph, *any boy would bring his mother back.* Ah—there it was. He felt some weight evaporate, foolishness constrict. Of course, his mother was his motivation. No reason to evade the truth—right?

"You worry you shame her memory," said the voice. *"But you know she would do the same for you."*

The Hounds of Gil'an Mor had most certainly possessed the intellect and technology to rewrite to history once upon a time—but would his mother have done the things that Geph had? Committed such atrocities? What he recalled of her said otherwise. But, then again, he never could have imagined himself as he was now. Not in all his years had Geph foreseen such bleakness, such a swift and horrid transformation of himself.

But maybe this is who I always was.

So many threads of possibility streaming from that thought. Geph pushed them away. Bad to dwell on such a notion now.

Reclamation, despite so many moving parts, so many sinhounds, was a rather solitary undertaking. It had been days since Geph had caught scent of his dark brethren—this was typical; there was much to raze and many a soul upon which to feast. Geph shuddered. Disgust churned in his gut, and he swallowed the urge to retch at the thought of such slaughter. What was the point? What reason had they for such rampant destruction? If Hush was to remake the world, rewrite histories wronged, was such... *barbarism* necessary?

"Sinhounds, Gephorax—we sniff out and eradicate excessive sin wherever it may be. It is in our very nature," said the voice. The fur along Geph's spine stood on end. The voice chuckled. *"As I said the night Helveden fell, there is false sin—excessiveness—and there is* true *sin. We are requisite. We are tempered sin, given leash enough to sate our hunger, but not so much we lose control."*

You and I, perhaps, thought Geph. *But what about the others?*

"Time will tell," the voice said. *"You will know — trust me."*

Underlight. Vast nothingness. Rock and ruin kissed by shadows, sick from darkness and millennia of solitude. Occasional snaps of light. Sad. Dim. Whispers of the distant past swimming aimlessly and biting at his ears. Ouran felt cold in his heart and bones. Whatever it was that kept him here, dragged him on through silent, phantom horror, he prayed he found it soon lest madness keep him here forever as its pet.

How long had he been walking? How far had he gone? Straight. Straight. He furled his wings about him tighter; the feathers shone warmly before their brilliance was devoured, plunging Ouran into nothingness once more. Was this place trying to tell him something, or was it trying to slowly feed of him? What, exactly, was Underlight? Where?

"It is only as dark as you allow to be," said a voice. Firm, measured. Everywhere. "It can taste your shame—are you truly so devoid of hope?"

Ouran stopped. "Who are you?"

"Many things to many people," it said. "Many a lost soul has come to Underlight—I provide them solace whether living or deceased." Ouran felt—thought he felt—a gentle hand caress his cheek. "What, weary wanderer, do you long for?"

So much. There was so much he—

She came to him as if a memory from a dream, his Sonja Lúm-talé. He could feel the darkness of Underlight enfolding him, constricting him, yet his eyes saw only her, backdropped by the city Banerowos, spires rising, glinting like a thousand distant, monstrous teeth. She extended him her hand.

"Is this... real?" Ouran whispered. Lump in his throat. Hot tears welling in his eyes. When last he had seen her, she had been a monstrous, vengeful thing in Hang-Dead Forest. A rusalk born of violent death. "Please—what is this?"

She took his hand, led him to the center of the spire city.

Dissolved to nothingness and took the gilded memory of Banerowos.

Ouran gasped as the darkness lifted, as the weight vanished and he found himself within the center of a city, yes— but not Banerowos. Something else entirely—a cavern city built into the rock walls of Underlight, architecture rough yet gentle. Motes of light flittered through the air; whispers swam about, lingering like a favorite song. In the distance stood a grand flight of stairs, atop which sat a temple. Ouran walked, spellbound, desperate.

"What is this?" he inquired once more. "What are—" Souls, he realized of the motes of light, the whispers. "Gods…" So much weight. Felt his lungs would burst. Just breathe. Fucking breathe. Panic welling, breathing quick and short. Was she here, his Sonja? He ascended the stairway with hastened, clumsy steps. Almost tripped a few times.

Being draped in light. Wings. Eyes the blue of a clear sky reflected in the sea.

"Welcome," it said, "to the city Seleneth. I am Irgi, Warden of Souls." Its voice was softer in such proximity. So gentle… calming. "I have long been expecting you—but by what name shall I call you? You have worn many…"

You have worn many… Ouran shuddered. He could tell this entity knew. There was a nonchalance to its upright posture, to the softness with which it spoke that, despite mollifying him slightly, also set him on edge. Made him feel naked, bones exposed—*soul* exposed.

"I…"

"*Second thoughts?*" Alerion asked.

Endless. Gods, but who was he? Ouran? Varésh? Alerésh or Dren? His skull screamed; he dug fingers into his scalp, biting back the urge the shriek at the pain. What was happening?

"Nameless," he uttered. Gods, but he didn't want to be *any of them.*

Irgi cocked its head. "I see." It approached, towered over Nameless by a head. Gazed into his eyes, its blue stare mesmerizing. Hand upon his cheek, a soft caress provoking tears and stripping him of mental and emotional weight. Nameless shuddered; he felt weak in the knees and allowed himself to collapse into Irgi's firm embrace and weep. Just stand there as rivulets of sorrow streamed slowly down his cheeks. Never had he felt so uncertain, so confused. Bare. Lacking in identity.

"A bed for the night, I think," said Irgi. "Rest in Seleneth will do you well."

Eyelids heavy. Shuddering yawn. Darkness. Nameless felt the Warden scoop him up into its arms. Warmth. A voice in his head, a whisper distant and inviting; leaves rattling in the wind.

Dusk in a meadow of tall grass.

Rain and a girl of light.

He had seen this all before.

Prelude

What an odd collection they four were. Two drenarians, a resurrected prince with a voice in his head, and a goddess. Avaria breathed deeply as they departed Nil-Illúm. Dark. Always dark, save the glow of a single illum wisp orbiting Fenrin. Avaria felt comfortable here, knew the feeling would fleet the further from the city they grew, for things beyond the walls of Nil-Illúm were never as they seemed; nothing in this world was, as Avaria had come to learn.

His thoughts drifted once more to Helveden, to his mother, Virtuoso Khal, and Norema. Gone. All of them. Wretched grin. Headless corpse. Avaria winced at the images, hissed through his teeth. They'd never fade, he knew, felt. Horrible tattoos. Chest stung, felt like a knife had been twisted in an open wound, plunged further. Fuck—they were gone. Dead.

Khal and Norema fell to the wayside and his mother occupied his thoughts wholly. His last words to her had been harsh; she had struck him across the face. That had been their final interaction. No pleasantries, no affection, no parting words of encouragement—just pain. Such had been their relationship soon after he'd been sent to the Hall. Pain and loathing, sorrow and loneliness. Fuck. The numbness of the past day thinned, waned, and tension gripped him wholly, squeezing like a serpent. It was going to be a long journey.

What if? The question dogged him as they walked. Nipped at his heels for hours on end. What if their last interaction had been different? Might it have changed the outcome; would she still be alive? What if Avaria had never departed Helveden to find the sword? Might Helveden yet remain? Might he have been able to stop Geph? What if?

What if?

What if?

What. Fucking. If.

"*Breathe*," said Jor. The measured softness of his tone snapped Avaria from thought and the cold dimness of the world provided him something other than retrospection to focus on.

I'm trying, Avaria thought. *It's difficult.*

"*I understand,*" said Jor. "*To recall such profound loss...*" There was something odd, reminiscent to the way he spoke. "*I too have lost much. I too have mourned. Before we two were one I dwelled in Gil'an Mor.*" He paused again. "*I... don't know how I remember that.*"

Something about death resetting things? Avaria asked. *You told me so the other day.*

"*This feels different,*" Jor said. "*Like a memory from a dream. Distant, yet so very vivid. The halls of Gil'an Mor were grand once. The streets were ripe with crystal. And in the Angelarium she sat—Ybot: Mother of Hounds, Reader of Time, First of Her Kind. The most graceful of them—of us—all.*"

The corner of Avaria's mouth twitched as an image of a winged hound manifested, lingered momentarily, then dispersed in specks of light in his mind. He blinked, briefly seeing stars. That had not been his memory, and he felt an ache in his chest, constricting. Mournful.

"*She was always kind to me,*" Jor said, a recollective airiness to the way he spoke. "*Treated me as... more than what I was.*" He sighed, and Avaria felt some of the tension flee, was able to breathe a little easier. "*The closest entryway to Underlight is through Gil'an Mor.*"

More ruins. Great.

"Gil'an Mor," Avaria said.

"What of it?" Luminíl asked.

"Is that where we're headed?"

"Yes," she said. She offered nothing more.

"Gil'an Mor," mused Fenrin. "What a relic."

"You know of it?" Avaria asked.

"Been there on several occasions," Fenrin said. "Dreams are interesting."

He too offered nothing more, and Avaria exchanged a brief glance with Erath, who simply shrugged. Her eyes betrayed her exhaustion. Why was she so tired? Not that Avaria blamed her—he was spent too, driven by adrenaline. But what had changed? Was it the radich she wielded now? He knew little about the energy other than the fact it allowed its wielder the ability to bend time, but he suspected there was so much more to it than that. It meant possibility, after all. Avaria fell back to walk in step with her.

"All right?" Stupid question. Erath quirked an eyebrow. Weary-eyed, but a smile played on her lips. "Yeah, me neither."

"I don't expect anyone would be after..." She sighed.

"Well, after all of this. Death. Destruction." Heavy eyelids. Distant sorrow swimming in her eyes. There was more than she was letting on.

Avaria squeezed her shoulder gently. "Won't press, but if you feel like talking…"

Erath nodded. "Thank you."

That was that. He understood. Had to gather yourself for the heavy things lest you crumble underneath the weight before you could get the words out.

Walk.

Silence.

Repeat.

How would this end? Erath couldn't help but linger on the question. So many variables. She swiped absentmindedly at the air, tore a momentary window to the past—to wherever. Too obscured to tell. Startling, nonetheless. It would be a while before this newfound gift—could she even call it that?—didn't make her jump every time she involuntarily used it. Gods… was this how the rest of her life would be, looking into memories and such with every gesture she made? She'd go mad if that were the case.

How long had they been at this? How far had they trekked? She knew the Peaks of Dren well enough, had explored their vastness over the years, yet she'd never been wherever it was they were now. Somehow, she'd managed to avoid it—or had *it* evaded her? Dead trees caked in rime. Spent glyphs and the ruin of myriad effigies—hounds had they been? Hard to tell given how far gone they were. Time and weather were gluttonous that way, feasting slowly on their meals, on whatever they saw fit.

"A prelude to the corpse of a once great city," Fenrin murmured. His fingers brushed along the effigies with gentle if not mournful reverence, and Erath wondered if perhaps these monuments were something more—*had been*, rather. "I dreamt of Gil'an Mor this walk. I see things even now." He held a hand to the air; faint threads of energy wreathed around his hand, snaked along his forearm.

Not energy, Erath realized, and Luminíl seemed to have taken notice too. A creature of a sort. Almost completely translucent save a pair of stark blue eyes.

"An Indrisori eel," Luminíl said. "This creature is foreign, of another world entirely." She frowned, looked at Erath with cold eyes. "Your radich is doing more than you are aware, girl. Pulling strings of its own accord."

"How do you know that?" Erath asked. Fenrin and Avaria looked to the Phoenix too. "What, actually, does that even mean?"

"You aren't entirely in control," Avaria said. "And radich *literally* means possibility, right? What if it's physically manifesting the past? Luminíl said the eel is alien to our world, and I suspect it's place of origin is..."

"Little more than a memory," Erath said. She felt a *tug* in the center of her chest; immense sorrow flooded through her, weighted her down, and she grabbed Fenrin's arm to steady herself. That had not been her emotion. Goose pimples rippled up her arms and neck at the possibility her body wasn't entirely her own.

"Gil'an Mor will test us all," Luminíl said as they started on their way. Snow and leafless trees. Weeping wind and muffled sobbing in the depths of Erath's mind.

The city wall appeared, gateless ingress warded over by a pair of towering hounds. Flee, they seemed to say, stay away from this awful place.

Or maybe it was the fear that had been festering in her for the past few days, emboldened, nourished by the woe and melancholy of the land and her companions.

They crossed the threshold.

Erath's memories wept.

EVERY INCH OF Avaria begged he flee this dead place as they descended into Gil'an Mor. A tomb of memories old and sad, all but lost to time save by those with long enough teeth or an allhound's presence in their mind.

A labyrinth of streets infected with the fissures and dead geodes. Old azure beneath their feet, wisps and threads of waning light adrift in the air, almost as if frozen in time. One brushed against Avaria's cheek and a shriek from the depths of his mind cleaved his skull in two. Felt like it had, at least. He doubled over, hissing through his teeth. Felt heavy.

"They are called Threads," Luminíl said, "and they are the memories of this place. Ghosts of longhounds past, bloated with the history of Gil'an Mor." Murmured, "And its violent end."

She held her hand to the Thread nearest Avaria and it came to her, snaked around her forearm, weak and slow. Mewed faintly at her presence and her touch.

"Sleep, now," the Phoenix whispered. She caressed the

spirit's length... and it fell to mist and motes of light. Vanished in the gloom of Gil'an Mor.

"What did you do?" Erath asked.

"Relieved its suffering," Luminíl said. "Took it for my own—the pain, that is." Such sorrow in her words. A hint of something dark. "Sometimes pain is the appropriate price." She looked to where the Thread had been just moments ago. "Her name was Alesana and she died when Hush attacked. The last to fall before they caged the Vulture in the depths of Underlight."

"A way to go before we reach Underlight," Fenrin said. "We had best move on." His upper lip curled slightly. "I do not like the air about this place, nor will I enjoy that about Underlight. The quicker we leave, the better."

They started on their way, Luminíl at the head and Fenrin taking up the rear. Something beautiful about ruins. Maybe it was the silence. Maybe it was the mystery of what had been.

"It is the connection," Jor said. *"The longing."*

How do you mean?

"Everyone connects to history in one way or another," Jor said. *"And whether or not they care to admit so, everyone desires adventure—longs for a taste of that which came before."*

215

Did you?

"*Of course,*" said Jor. "*Just as you do now. Your quest, in its simplest form, was born of a need, a desire to be free of the confines of Helveden. Now? Now, you seek that which came before.*"

Banerowos.

Avaria shivered at the city's name and knew that Jor was right. He had yearned for adventure for the longest time—but he hadn't thought that desperation would lead him here to the corpse of Gil'an Mor, or that his home would fall along the way, everyone and everything he'd known slaughtered. Little more than memories.

Mother...

They walked.

Sages

The village was called Yll and Geph was surprised it stood. Surprised that anything at all endured here in the vast sickness of the meadow. The village was an odd, gray amalgamation of leaning not-quite-towers and uneven buildings which looked as though they were all cobbled together from the ruin of much uglier things. And the smell—gods, what an unforgiving thing. Apple pie atop the odor of rotting flesh. Geph's stomach churned as he padded on his way.

Scarcely populated was Yll. By the time he reached the village square Geph had only seen a dozen or so finite occupants. They had paid him no mind; he was practically a ghost. While he should have been content with this invisibility of sorts, he was not. How long had it been since he had spoken with someone or something beside the voice in his head?

"Nice doggy."

Geph turned to the voice. Gaze fell on a dark-haired child with amber eyes and a grin. His nose twitched as the child approached. Without hesitation, he scratched *that spot* behind Geph's ears.

"Whatcha doin' here, doggy?"

Was an actual answer expected? Was the child aware of what Geph was?

"Passing through."

The child continued scratching. "To where?"

"A bad place. An old place."

"Why?"

"You would not understand, little one."

The child cocked an eyebrow. Stopped scratching. Frowned, turned and started off. Geph sighed. *Children.* Ears perked up. Something more than just a child—its shadow was *wrong;* met the light instead of fled.

Geph trailed the child-thing at a distance. The stench of Yll grew more profound with every step he took, with every corner that they turned, until Geph was sure he would be sick.

An ugly, twisted patchwork remnant of a tower greeted him, and the child-thing halted at its door. "Why do you follow, doggy?" Agitation.

"To converse," said Geph. "We both are more than we appear. I apologize for my dismissiveness. It was ignorant, and I wish to make amends."

The child-thing said nothing. Twitched a finger—they were in the tower, now. In the depths and darkness of a place that made Geph's neck fur bristle. Light was all but dead here, save the intermittent flickering of dying wisps.

Geph sneezed. A familiar and haunting scent.

"You reek of her," the child-thing said, abandoning all pretense of ignorance and youth. "Of the Vulture, Mirkvahíl."

"I do," said Geph. "What is she to you?"

"Can I show you something?" The child-thing turned and reached for Geph. Eyes like dying stars. Tapped his nose, and Geph was in the center of a ruin wreathed in wispy threads of smoke. Glass and stone hung in the air, ignorant of gravity; the entire ruin turned its nose to law.

A lanky shadow manifested several feet from Geph. "Misten Fahg was a place of power." Child-thing. "And then the Vulture came..."

THE DRENARIAN CITY is calm. For half a moment the stillness reminds Hush of home, and she longs for those evening walks by the lake. Just the two of them, she and Luminíl. But the feeling fades, slips away in the snowfall, and Hush is alone.

Loneliness tugs at her again, but this time Hush can feel it belongs to Te Mirkvahíl. Something about this place—some-*one*, perhaps. Many, in fact. She walks, each step as aimless as it is meaningful. What is this city and its people to Te Mirk-vahíl? What *was* it?

"Aveline." Hush turns to the voice, hardly of her own ac-cord; Te Mirkvahíl remains. A woman stands a yard or two away.

"My Queen Silith," Hush says. So many questions.

The drenarian queen nears Hush, bores into her with hawkish yellow eyes. She is beautiful, but she is worn. Wea-ry. Time is such a rotten thing, Hush thinks; she can feel the rot beneath her flesh, swimming in her heart and scraping through her mind.

Silith touches Hush's cheek. So tender. She can feel the queen's sorrow. She allows Silith to embrace her; reluctant-ly, Hush returns the gesture. It feels... nice, the firmness, the longing. It reminds her of Luminíl.

They pull apart. "I've not seen you since..." Silith sighs.

"Since Alor." The name *stings* Hush physically, and it's all she can do not to wince. "I thought you dead all this time. Once news reached of Te Mirkvahíl's demise..."

Hush cocks an eyebrow. Play the part. "You knew?"

"We *all* knew."

Borrowed shame. Hush hangs her head. Sighs.

"What is done, is done," Silith says. Touches Hush's cheek. "I would show you something if you'll follow. Something of Alor's."

Hush nods of her own volition, pushes back against the will of Te Mirkvahíl. Humor the queen. Play the part, for all things have their use.

Silith takes her hand. They twist through the drenarian city and out into the trees, their mountain kingdom kissed by mist like darkness and a silence eager to infect what little sanity of Hush remains.

"What a thing to admit," the voice inside her says. Hush says nothing; the voice does not relent. *"Pertinent, for no one sane could do what we have done. Too much fear. A lack of passion. Loveless, wretched things."*

A totem in a glade. An effigy of something long and winged. Hush has seen these many times before; they are strewn about this dying world of hers. Its very presence stings her borrowed flesh.

She screams.

Has been screaming for so long.

Silith kneels beside her, eyes aglow like dying moons, lips drawn to a thin line upon which Hush smells blood and rage and woe.

Smoke. Her flesh is burning.

Burning.

BURNING

and she wails—

not this place again.

"YOU HAD THE dreams again, didn't you?"

Rhona stood atop the tallest spire in all Banerowos. Below her were miles of ruin. Before her stood Djen, pale flesh cracked and webbed with mirkúr.

"This is the dream," said Rhona.

Djen frowned. "Have you truly learned nothing from all of this? How many more times will we repeat this song and dance? How much longer do you intend to run?"

"I'm not running," Rhona said.

"You *are*." Djen held her arms out wide. "In circles. How

many times have you escaped this place only to have it draw you back? The guilt will always call you back if you allow it to." She approached Rhona. Cupped her cheeks. "Is this what you want to be?"

Tears. Hot.

"Stop."

"Answer the question."

Rhona screamed. Shrieked, and the force of her anguish sent Djen sailing through the air and off the edge of the spire. Fragments of the gray sky fell like sheets of ash. Rhona fell to her knees, sobbing. She could hear them as they manifested, neared at gentle glides—myriad shadows of self. A cacophony of chaos somewhere in between a whisper and a hiss.

"*Wake.*"

"*Rouse, before you kill them all.*"

"*Feed.*"

"*You are more. You are better than the cracked and broken shell you wear.*"

"*Feed.*"

"*Rend. Feast. Sleep.*"

Wet hand. Warm. Rhona blinked.

* * *

SO MANY DEAD. So much blood.

So many body parts strewn across the glade.

Her hand is warm and slicked with blood—Silith's blood. And her mouth... Hush retches, wills her tongue to kill the taste of iron. Begs her sense of smell and taste to die.

The drenarian queen is dead. Dead dead dead.

Dead.

Hush screams—almost. Swallows the shriek; her insides burn like the hell she has wrought. How many times must she dream and wake and dream and wake and—-

She pushes herself to stand. Stumbles forward. Who knows where? Just away. Get away get away get away. Such a cracked and broken thing.

I will make this right. I will fix it all.

How many times has she told herself that lie?

She bites back tears.

Help.

"WHAT IS THIS place?" Geph asked. "What are you?"

"A monster," said the child-thing. "I am a monster, and this is my home."

"Might you care to elaborate? You called this place Misten

Fahg."

"The tower at the center of the village Sleep," said child-thing. "When they say, 'I am going to sleep,' this is where they come—Misten Fahg. The epicenter of The In Between."

"So, you are quite literally a thing of dreams," said Geph. He inched closer, intrigued. "But what is Mirkvahíl to you? And what is Misten Fahg to her?"

Child-thing sneered. The silhouette flared. "As without, so within. Mirkvahíl brought ruin to your world, but what she did to Misten Fahg was far more monstrous. She *created Hell*. Perdition. Down Below. Call it what you will—her cowardice infected *all*." The silhouette recoiled. "I was beautiful once. The Dream Wolf, they called me. Time."

Geph frowned. Ears twitched. He felt sympathy for this strange, canine soul. "And now—what do they call you?"

A twist of shadow. A trembling of ruin. A black wolf, eyes like dying stars and a form that trailed to mist. "Than Sor'Al."

Wide-eyed. Bristling fur. Geph bowed deeply. He was in the presence of a god-thing. "Great One," he whispered. "You humble me. My mother told me tales of you when I was but a pup. I never thought... You are *real*."

"The most monstrous things are often times hidden in the

subtext of a child's tale," said Than Sor'Al. "Such little nightmares do I bring…."

"What do you wish of me?" Geph asked. "Why show me Misten Fahg?"

"As without, so within," repeated Than Sor'Al. "Mirkvahíl is such an old and splintered soul. A tower at its tipping point, so to speak. One need only give a little push—"

Geph howled himself awake. Found himself in tall grass beneath a sea of stars. Trembling like mad. That had all been… *real*—hadn't it? His skull ached horribly, like it'd been split in two, and he couldn't quell the distant whisper—"*One need only give a little push.*" Had this anything to do with what he'd seen of Hush's memories? That strange and twisted place called Hang-Dead Forest. Banerowos.

"*Get up, Gephorax,*" said the voice in his head. "*Get up and walk.*"

So, he did.

And the night endured.

NAMELESS WOKE TO pale blue light and a feeling of absence in his head. No—not absence. Intrigue? That didn't sound right either. Nagging? Caged chaos?

"Amnesia," said Alerion. *"Selective amnesia."*

No use in asking what he'd voluntarily banished from his mind. Though how he'd done so... Nameless recalled nothing past the Warden Irgi placing him in bed. Emptiness, then pale blue light; now.

He slipped from bed, garbed as he had been prior to his sleep, and instinct drew him back to the staircase atop which he had first encountered Irgi in the city Seleneth. The Warden was there when Nameless arrived, its aura of nonchalance doing more to rattle Nameless than to ease his nerves. What was it about this entity that cause him such distress? Those eyes, bright as a blue sky echoed by the sea. Wise in a way that made him shiver, for why should anything know more about a person than a person knew about themself?

"You are a man of many lives," said Irgi. "Yet you acknowledge none—are you truly so controlled by fear and guilt? By fear *of* guilt?"

"I want to be a blank canvas," Nameless said.

"Many do," said Irgi. "But tell me—how can you be a blank canvas when you're haunted by the unknown? You let sleep take from you the source of your suffering, yet now you suffer, and you can't say why."

Weight. Tightening chest.

"Repression is intoxication without a drink," said Irgi. "It will destroy you from the inside out unless you face your fears. What is the saying? The guilt will always call you back. The longer you run, the worse it will be." The Warden bent over, leaned in close. "And you have been running for *such* a long time."

Hot tears. Burning, like a fire in his chest. Cracks in the tapestry of his mind; lost things aching to be remembered.

"How do I fix this?" Nameless whispered.

Portal of azure luminescence. Gossamer threads of light. A voice beyond it all. "Hell is a place of one's own making."

Seleneth dissolved, fell away in rivulets of muted color; with the cavern city went its host, and there was only Nameless and a brilliant doorway at the center of a vast and endless blackness. Nameless blinked. Was he dreaming? Had he died? The portal shimmered, shifted, and he saw a meadow of tall grass. Beyond it...

"Hang-Dead Forest."

Nameless stepped through the portal

and found himself lying on his back.

Starlight blinked.

A feeling in his chest.

Parable.

Underlight

Ouran'an was dead. Had been for a time. The city stood in the distance like the jagged, snow-tipped maw of some gargantuan beast. It was not the first of its kind to fall, and Avaria knew it would not be the last.

How did he know that?

He blinked. Gulped the crisp air of this place now called the Deep Rock as he gazed at Ouran'an. It beckoned, and he longed to walk its streets, to stand atop its many spires and kiss the morning sky.

But why?

Blink.

Such a ruin. Such a sorry thing the city was. Streets of blackened bones encased in ice. Threads of mirkúr coiling through the air like rivulets of angry fog. A breeze like knives against his flesh. Swore it'd raised the dead for he could hear the countless screams entwined with grief and joy like some abomination wrought in Hell.

Blink.

Ghosts. Aimless wanderers where in life they'd walked with purpose, for Reshapers and their magics were how so much of Harthe was wrought.

Hand to his head—how had known that?

"Bzzz." Sentience in a sea of silent resignation. "Bzzzz." Avaria searched for the master of the voice like gravel tossed by waves. Again—"Bzzz."

A swirl of mist, a snap of light; he was elsewhere now. Before him stood a man. What had been a man, at least, for mirkúr streaked his flesh, trailed beyond the realm of physicality, dancing in the wind. He was blond of hair, lithe, with arms and shoulders graced by intricate tattoos. His eyes were white and Avaria felt the stranger's gaze *inside his mind*.

"Stop." He retreated half a step.

"Bzzz." The man cocked his head. "Bzzz."

"No," Avaria said. "I've no idea why I'm here, let alone how I arrived. Don't know who you are either—*get out* of my head!"

Mirkúr flared inside Avaria; a short sword manifested in his hand. Jagged. Nasty. Hungry. He pointed the tip of the blade at the man.

The man held his hands up. "Bzzz." Half-turned, pointed to an archway and the many hills beyond, up from which an endless throng of tombstones rose.

"The burial grounds?" Avaria held his stance. "Why?"

"Bzzz," the man said softly. Turned and started on.

Blink.

Ouran'an had never had burial grounds.

Blink.

An oak tree cloaked in snow. Beneath it stood the man. Beyond it, thing of wings and shadow. They beckoned; Avaria obeyed.

"WHERE WILL YOU go?"

"East. I think."

"Are you not happy here?"

"It has nothing to do with happiness."

"What, then?"

"Dreams. I thought you of all people would understand." Silence. "You saved me, raised me as your own and I am grateful—but my purpose lies beyond this place of rock and snow and death."

"Death is inescapable."

"But slaughter can be quelled."

"Yes...."

Calm snow. Sky of trees.

So cold.

"Do you not love us, Erath?"

Erath sits against the trunk of a tree. It is spring and the air is sweet though momentarily poisoned by the inquiry. She looks at Alor. "Of course, I do. Why would I not?"

Alor says nothing.

"You let us die," Leru says. She sits at Erath's left. A shadow falls across the world and chokes away spring. All becomes cracked and withered, dry and dead like grass that's gone millennia without rain. "You let us die to sate your insecurities."

A twist of smoke and a snap of light. They are standing now in Nil-Illúm.

"Middle child, lost and full of woe," the specter of Alor taunts. She is naught but incorporeal burnt-paper flesh and ravenous eyes like dying stars. She trails to nothingness, to the planes beyond with every step she takes. Leru is her half-head shorter shadow twin.

"What will father think?" Leru inquires.

"What will mother think?" Alor hisses.

Erath trembles. "I…" She what? Did not mean to let her sisters die? To let the monsters of the world slaughter them? "I'm so sorry.…"

Screaming snow.

"You are a cruel girl," Queen Silith whispers in her ear.

Erath starts, spins. "Mother…"

"Our girls," her father, Fenrin, murmurs and his eyes are red. "Your sisters… How could you, Erath?" Her heart stings: they four encircle her like the wolves to her trembling lamb. Fenrin weeps. "You are no daughter of mine."

Erath falls to her knees, hugs herself, bites back tears, swallows a sob.

Hand on her shoulder. Gentle voice in her ear. "The guilt will always call you back, dear girl." Dren, glorious and sad. "And such a monstrous thing it is, especially when we know there is nothing more we could have done."

Erath leans into Dren. Traitorous, mad Dren. The only thing here that feels safe. The tempest of emotion circling

Erath slows, as if time itself desires sleep. Motes and threads of soft blue light flitter through the air, caress Erath as they pass.

"I can help you from this awful place," says Dren. He stands, pulling Erath upright. "I can help you gain control. You *must* gain control if you are to upset the sickness." He sighs. "Underlight is such a twisted place..." He snaps his fingers and the two stand 'neath an archway warded over by a pair of effigies that Erath does not recognize. Winged, face-less things; four-armed, wielding blades. Beyond the arch-way, stones of light; a pathway leading elsewhere, from here, somewhere new.

"A word of advice," says Dren, taking Erath's hand. "Nothing in this place—nothing in this world—is as it seems. There is truth in madness and madness in truth. We must find the balance in between."

They walk and the stones shimmer.

They walk and the air chills

screams

weeps.

Gods, what is this place? So beautiful and twisted. Swirls of ruin in a sky of colors Erath cannot name. Blinks of places elsewhere, somehow, somewhen, beyond comprehension.

"Somewhere in the midst of all this," Dren says. "Balance."

Snap.

All dilates.

Contracts.

Snap.

Tower ruin. Glass and stone adrift, suspended in the air.

"How many masks will you wear? How many times will you stain this place with your presence, Varésh Lúm-talé?" something growls. "Speak, or I will consume you and the flesh you wear."

What did it—

"I come seeking balance," Erath says, but it is not her voice she hears. She feels wings protruding from her back, feels her bones reshape; she is on fire, burning from the inside out as Varésh Lúm-talé—whomever that is—takes her body for his own. So much guilt inside this flesh. Infection. Plague. Were she in control she would retch.

"You helped her destroy this place," the entity snarls. Manifests—black wolf. Eyes like dying stars and a shape that fades to mist. "Who are you to enter Sleep and make demands?"

Varésh Lúm-talé sighs. "I have made many mistakes." He

locks eyes with the wolf. "Please, great Than Sor'al. If not for me then for the soul with whom I trek. She has suffered much to reach this place." Whispers, "*I have caused her so much pain...*"

Than Sor'al snorts. It clouds before the beast's nose. "Release her from your flesh that she might manifest before me."

Varésh nods.

Blink.

Erath starts. Than Sor'al's nose is cold, makes her shiver as it sniffs her up and down.

"Radich," says the wolf, with a hint of disdain. Bows its head. "What a cruel thing you are, Varésh Lúm-talé, to have tainted her with such a thing. You and your many names, your countless, rotten iterations. How many times until you learn? How many more worlds condemned to wither 'neath the consequences of your desperate guilt?" Starlight eyes burn red. "Leave us."

Blink.

Erath stands beside the massive wolf in the blasted remnant of a town on either side of which the tower and a forest loom. "Sleep is not what it once was," Than Sor'al laments, "but I shall do my best."

Blink.

CALM SNOW. OAK tree rearing in the night.

Sky of trees. Buzzing man. Thing of wings and shadow. Cricket serenade; the biting cold inside his flesh. He cries and it is small and desperate. Man and shadow watch but do not move. He is weak. So frighteningly weak. His tiny frame is fading, losing to the dark and snow. Won't somebody—

A forest cloaked in mist, the melody of distant death. He is older now yet haunted by the dreamlike memory of that night. Or a memory like a dream. Nothing in this world makes sense, not when he can summon beasts of Hell. Not when he's been banished to the Hall, the fucking lot of good that's done. Erudition and achievement are the falsities that ward the truth—the Hall is where they murder happiness, mold abandoned boys to function as the tools that drive their wars. Fuck Helveden. Fuck Ariath. Fuck—

He hugs her tightly. How many nightmares must a little boy endure before the gentleness of dreamless sleep takes hold? How many times must he relive that wicked night inside the woods? Cold and dark and snow.

"You are safe," she whispers. "Safe and warm and found

and I will never let you go."

"What if the darkness tries to take me back?" he whispers.

She pulls him closer, kisses his forehead. "It will meet my blade."

He sniffles. "And if it takes you instead?"

"It won't."

THEY ARE ALL of them dead. He remembers little save the shadow from the forest of trees and spire rocks. It came, and Ouran'an fell. It came, and they went—his memories and the people whom the city housed.

Everything has led him here—but why? What is left in the shadow of a ruin, of a distant memory, for him to find?

You know, the sky says. *You have always known.*

Scenery of three lives stitched together over one another like a mangled corpse with mismatched parts. The triptych melds and the sky is black despite the blazing sun. They stand there, boy and hound and man, eyes fixed knowingly on one another.

"Why have you forsaken us?"

They turn, do boy and hound and man, come face to face with individuals who stoke in them a tempest of irrationality and rage and grief.

"Mother..." breathe the boy and hound, withering in the presence of a thing of starlight eyes and tattered wings and a woman red of hair and wielding mirkúr blades.

The man says nothing as he looks upon the queen.

A grin rips across her face; a cackle-shriek erupts.

Chaos.

SLEEP IS DEAD. Beyond dead. Erath trails Than Sor'al. How does any of this relate to balance? How will wandering through this corpse of stone contribute to her gaining dominance of her radich, weird and poisoned power that it is? What is Than Sor'al? Erath hugs herself for warmth; this place is cold. Beautiful. Haunting. Every step she takes pulls back the curtain just a little more. Screams and whispers, fleeting visions of... what?

"You reek of chaos," Than Sor'al says. "Chaos and fear."

"I'm scared," Erath says. "Afraid to fail. Of... all of this."

"Balance is not easily achieved," says Than Sor'al. They stop at the edge of a silver lake in which the cosmic brilliance of the sky reflects. "Were it so, perhaps then Sleep and Misten Fahg might rise anew. As without, so within—ruin."

"You speak simply," Erath says, "but there is a deeper meaning to your words. This place is a reflection of the waking world, isn't it? An analog of sorts."

"Clever girl."

Erath kneels before the lake, gazes in at her reflection.

The wind whispers in her ear; she shrugs it off. It will not relent.

They come from all around, manifest from nothing like a million waking stars. Motes and threads, a brilliant symphony. They encircle Erath, pull her to her feet. Whispers like a song she swears she's heard before.

Whispers like a dying voice.

A resurgent voice.

Her eyes are wide; she understands.

"Please," she asks of Than Sor'al, "deliver me from Sleep." The light-song caresses Erath's mind. Something in her snaps, surges, awakens. "I can save them yet."

"As you—"

A CITY SLEEPS. They safely sleep.

The Phoenix. The Father-king.

The Prince of Countless Names is gone.

"Peel back the fabric of the world," says a gentle voice. Winged figure wrought of light. "Every moment bends beneath your will."

"How will I know?" Erath asks.

"Follow the light. Close your eyes and follow the light."

THERE.

WAIT—WAIT!

So close.

TOO FAR. TOO far.

Peel it back.

Follow the light. Follow the thread.

Oh gods...

HE WAKES IN the amalgam of the cities he has known. They are a crush of ruined, crooked stone and twisted spires rising at impossible, if not unnatural angles. Gossamer threads of pitch swim through the air with the lethargy of basking snakes; the sky is red, the moon sits high and black, a dilated pupil-of-a-thing. His skin crawls; his mind screams, each

243

shriek less intelligible than the last.

Toll the Hounds. Their cries descend, directionless, without origin. He makes no move to flee; he waits—sin is relentless. The amalgam shifts: the scenery bleeds and he is standing at the gates of Ouran'an. The city is a monument to failure, the roost of desecration. His heart aches to see it, dead and silent; he flees the necropolis he once called home—

Cold. Can scarcely breathe. Rocks and snow. So horribly alone. Best to lay here, die. Fade to memory like the rest.

A shadow thing of wings. Beautiful, a thing conceived of woe and dread, colder than the darkest night; in comparison, the snow and rocks are warm. Waning world, he sees their faces in his dreams, yearns to hold their hands; he is but a boy.

Gentle hands. A dark embrace: the longing floods him.

He will live.

WHAT A DEAD world.

"HERE YOU ARE again."

Wings of midnight feathers, tapering into mist. Eyes like summer storms. The night is blood; the grass is dead. Save the gnarled and twisted tree, they are alone.

Avaria clasps his hands behind his back, walks past Alerion to the tree. Lost Tree. Memory, Sorrow, Thorn. Bringer. He caresses Bringer's bark and the dream world fluctuates, the great tree groans.

"It took me a while to understand," Avaria says. "I have been asleep a very long while, trapped in memories, manifesting dread, letting anger feast upon me as it's wont to do."

"You know then they are dead," Alerion says. "Those with whom you ventured into Underlight. The world is dead, and you are here."

"Luckily, *here* is not yet dead. Nor is the world." He kisses Bringer; white light threads the ancient bark. Rejuvenates. Leaves stretch from infancy; they shimmer. Bringer sighs.

"*How?*" the tree inquires.

Saplings rise. The sky congeals; the blood-night fades to ash, reveals the soothing colors of a setting sun. Virgin stars have roused.

"You," Avaria says. "Bringer—the very illum network itself." He breathes deeply of the fresh air. "I told myself that death has a funny way of piecing things together. It just takes time."

Alerion nods. "Well done, Jor."

A shiver up his spine. It's been so long since Avaria has been called by that name. The memories snap, flash on repeat—cities, death, and cold.

"Mother," he whispers, and he thinks of Aveline and Hush. Of Ahnil and her maddened grin. "How I failed you all..." Three dead, one beyond redemption. He sits.

"What now?" Alerion asks.

Avaria shuts his eyes. "We wait."

Act III

O, Catastrophe

Bleak

ost. So incredibly lost. How could things have gone so wrong?

Erath kicked the dirt of the dead world in which she stood. A blanket of ugly night devoid of stars. A deafening silence and a wind that sliced at her with every dry gust. The stumps of myriad trees checkered the world, wherever and whenever she was.

And how was she going to get back to Underlight? To Luminíl and Fenrin—to the Phoenix and her *father*. Gods, what a mess. She swallowed the lump in her throat—do *not* lose composure.

Breathe. Balance. Find it, cage it. Otherwise, what was the point of any this? What had the point of this nightmare been if she gave up now?

But it would be so easy, a part of her thought. *Just sit here in the darkness. Let the world corrode—let them* all *wither, fade to ash.*

LUKE TARZIAN

Timelessness.

Time meant nothing.

The eternal yawn.

She screamed

...

...

...

Again.

A shimmer in the gloom. A twist of light.

"Why do you despair?" a voice inquired. Erath blinked; before her stood a man. A ghost of a man. A ghost of a memory of a man. Something. "Erath?"

She started at her name.

At the caress of her cheek. His hand was warm.

"I'm so lost," she whispered. The emotional weight was banging at the chamber door. "Lost and... Is this just a nightmare? Am I dead? Is this where my soul is fated to remain?"

"What do you believe?" the man asked.

She didn't know.

He asked again.

Still, she didn't know.

He wilted; the darkness ate his light, and the barren earth

consumed his corpse.

She was alone.

So

utterly

...

alone.

SHE HAD COME so close so many times—yet Avaria had not been able to reach her. Waiting had not meant inaction; rather, it had meant patience until the moment presented itself, and so many moments there had been.

"She is stuck," he said to Bringer and Alerion.

"Perhaps it was too much to expect a novice wielder of radich to find us here," Alerion said. "Trapped in the Temporal Sea..."

"No," Avaria said. "She wields it for a reason. I think..." He frowned, winced at a sharpness in his chest; his corporeality fluctuated. "Her anchor wanes."

Fuck.

"If that happens..." Alerion sighed. "Then you die. We die. She remains adrift and the world whence you came fades to ruin."

"So, what do we do?" Avaria asked.

Alerion frowned. "We wait. We hope."

HUSH RETCHES BLOOD. Retches something. Spews rot and bile and woe until her stomach is a growling pit. The abyss from which her hunger manifests to ruin worlds.

Worlds. Obscured images snap across her mind. Her sense of smell is overcome with scents from days dead and those yet to arrive. She falls to her knees; she can scarcely catch her breath, collect herself. She feels the old dry grass between her fingers and its touch sparks dread—the rot of Banerowos has a long reach. The dead have memories longer yet. She trembles, struggles to steel herself in such proximity to the ruined city and the forest behind which it remains.

"*Are you going to give up?*" the voice inside her asks. It goes by Mirkvahíl now. Mirkvahíl, who betrayed her lovely Luminíl, who with the liar Varésh Lúm-talé condemned the city Banerowos and its people to their ends. Who like so many others things in Hush's life was just a lie. A conglomerate of falsities.

So many lies.

"*So close,*" Mirkvahíl hisses.

When did Hush become this *thing?* How did she allow this monster to regain its foothold in her mind? *Weak,* she laments. *I am forever weak*

"*But you can be strong,*" Mirkvahíl urges. "*You can rectify it all—every broken world erased... You can save your love before it all goes wrong.*"

Snap.

So many trees.

Hush trembles. Tears well. Her jaw quivers.

Not here—not again.

THE MEADOW AT the end of time—that was all this was. It would have sounded more poetic had it not frightened Erath. How far had she gone? How long had she been at this? Where was the light, her guide? Follow the light. Gods, she couldn't even do *that* properly.

She dropped to the dead earth and screamed, pounded the dirt with her fists. Pull back the curtain of world—ha! She had done that, all right, and look where it had gotten her. What a fool she had been to think she could wield radich. What a fool she had been to think she could save it all, *them* all. Her shoulders slumped. She sniffled.

"Oh Avaria... Where are you?"

A sign. Something. Anything. The utter silence of this place tore at her. An endless night, a silence in black and white. She heaved a ragged sigh, forced herself to stand. She was empty, emptier than she had ever felt. Doing this, this... world-hopping, reality-swimming, whatever it was, drained her like nothing else had, fed on more than just simple stamina. This was more than exhaustion.

"...anchor wanes..."

Erath blinked. She had heard that, hadn't she?

"...wait... hope..."

Words like a whisper amid turning pages.

A twinkle, a luminescent dot so far away it may as well have not existed—-yet in the darkness here the brilliance blazed. Her father had always said that in the darkest night, the faintest light was blinding. She was the moth to its innumerable snapping flames.

Snap.

"...gone ...all gone..." Weeping. "...please..."

Snap.

She dug deep, called—begged what little she had left. Feet ached. Heart stung. Blood and breath so cold she felt the kiss of fire. Her very *existence* fluctuating—yes, that was it. Could feel her tethers to the place whence she had come evaporating, splitting like dry strands of hair.

Had to reach that light.

Snap.

Snap.

Snap.

SNAP.

"Erath?"

Yore

Hang-Dead Forest smelled of her, and she reminded him of home—of the home that once had been. Nameless trembled at the memories, at her phantom touch within his mind, pulling, tugging, clawing. Atrocities.

He walked, a pitiful sack of fear and adrenaline, remorse and self-loathing. The corpses and the ropes from which they'd hung had faded long ago, but Nameless felt their presence nonetheless—nothing ever truly left Hang-Dead Forest, the accursed place it was. He was proof enough that guilt would always call you back.

He stopped in a grove illuminated by the muted glow of the moon. At its center stood the woman he had once called wife—what was left of her at least. Hung those countless centuries ago, returned to haunt the forest as a rusalk. She eyed him.

"Sonja," he rasped. Shivered at the myriad eyes blooming

in the darkness behind her. "After all this time..."

"*Why have you come?*" Her voice was dry wind.

"To fix things," he said. "To fix myself, I think."

Sonja snarled. "*You are beyond repair.*"

She had attacked him when last he'd come. When he had been Varésh Lúm-talé. Was his abandoning of the name the reason why she held her ground, why the others like her made no move to rip him limb from limb? He clenched his teeth at the exhumed memory; threads of history were seeping through the cracks of his mind. Burning like cold fire.

"Maybe," he murmured. "What should I do?"

"*Have honor for once,*" Sonja said. "*Be brave.*" She turned to the trees. "*Atop her throne sits Mother Sin, the Ruin Queen. If whatever it is you are has any remorse, confront the demoness and free us from this hell.*"

Nameless nodded. "I will try."

Sonja eyed him; for a moment, her eyes were gentle. "*You will. You are not Varésh.*"

She withdrew from the glade and melded with the trees; one by one, the faceless eyes fell silent. Nameless was alone.

So, he walked.

* * *

A BREEZE. THE air was warm and gentle on her cheeks; the sunset and the rousing stars adorned the sky, and the light and colors did not burn. The sensation was so jarringly wonderful Erath almost forgot someone had called her name. She blinked. A short distance away stood a grand tree and two figures, one regal and winged, the other placid and wreathed with intricate tattoos. She recognized them both to a degree.

"Dren? Avaria?"

"Almost," the winged man said. "I am Alerion."

She looked at the tattooed man. "And you?"

"Avaria," he said. Smiled. "You found me. Us."

Darkness snapped across her memory. She hugged herself. "I was afraid I wasn't going to." Felt that sharp tug at the center of her chest. Winced. "I can't stay much longer."

"Your tether is waning," Avaria said. "We should go."

So tired. Gods, she was exhausted. Sweat dripping down her face. Avaria caught her as she slumped forward, kept her on her feet. *Focus. Grab the light.* She urged her radich, reached inside herself to stoke the energy into action; its signature was faint. *Just one more time...*

Her flesh bloomed; rivulets of pale blue luminescence manifested in her veins. Threads of mist braided outward, wreathing her and Avaria, enfolding and depositing them elsewhere—elsewhen.

The odor of ancient rot snapped her to her senses.

"Banerowos," Avaria murmured. Then, to himself: "Farewell, Alerion. Bringer."

He had clearly not expected *this* to have transpired so quickly; Erath felt a minuscule pang of guilt, but it was banished by a throng of disembodied screams and a maddeningly quick succession of Dren's memories as her radich ripped the veil apart. So many dead. So much woe. Gods, the anguish burned her from the inside out.

Her breath was shaky, but she forced herself to gulp the sick air and steady her nerves. "The guilt will always call you back," she whispered; the words were addressed to what remained of Dren.

"Where are Luminíl and Fenrin?" Avaria asked.

She'd nearly forgotten about them. "Underlight last I was aware, but..." Erath shook her head. "Everything is chaos; I can hardly make sense of anything. They may still be in Underlight, or somewhere else entirely."

Avaria frowned. "We can't take her just the two of us." He meant Hush. His eyes narrowed and his tattoos shone faintly in the gloom. "There's something else here. Some*one* else." He inhaled. Tensed his jaw. "More than one."

GEPH RETCHED. NO idea how long he'd been lost in Hang-Dead Forest. No idea how long his mind and nerves had been subjected to the remnant woe and anguish of this awful place. He shook violently as the hot sick dripped from his tongue and smacked the dirt. Gods, what he would do for a whiskey and a lack of smell…

Nose twitched. Geph composed himself as best the forest-eyes and city-corpse allowed. Others here. Familiar and not. His ears twitched and his forehead drew taught with shame. Avaria was somewhere near—how could he look him in the eyes? How could he speak to him after… Geph may not have spilled her blood, but he had bayed the sinhounds into action. Helveden and Ahnil were on Geph's paws and conscience. Could he bring himself to fight back if Avaria came at him, tried to kill him?

"You did what was necessary, Gephorax." Still had no idea what that voice was. *"There is a reason for everything."*

And what, pray tell, is that? Why did Ahnil Norrith and the city Helveden have to die?

"*Patience, Gephorax,*" the voice urged. "*All shall be revealed.*"

Geph snarled. *Does that include you?* Would that he could, he'd have ripped the voice from his head so that it might manifest and perish by his bite.

The voice chuckled. "*Slow for such a cunning thing. You and I, Gephorax, are one and the same. I am the courage you concealed, freed and fed by Hush. You know this, but you fear it, as you have feared so many things in all your years.*"

The air around Geph chilled. An inky blackness manifested through the folds of reality, and Geph found himself standing face to face with a wolf with eyes like dying stars.

"*How long do you intend to run?*" said Than Sor'al "*How long do you intend to sleep?*"

Distant voices. Trembling world.

They called his name.

"*The guilt will always call you back,*" said Than Sor'al. "*Embrace it and be free.*"

The world shattered.

Myriad fragments.

A thousand shards like broken memories and dreams.

"*They call me Time,*" said a voice.

Said Geph, and the black-eyed woman smiled.

* * *

"YOU HAD BETTER not be dead," Avaria snarled. Geph was motionless. The night about them screamed. "You're not allowed to die like this, damn it. Not until…"

Until, what? Until he had beaten the longhound senseless for his mother and Helveden? Until he had killed Geph, only to resurrect him for a second throttling? Avaria sighed, felt the hatred dissipate at the sight of Geph, still and silent as a drowned pup. He picked the longhound up, cradling him; he was surprisingly light.

"What did this to him?" Erath asked.

"This place," Avaria said. The sway and sentience of the corpse of Banerowos made no efforts to conceal itself. It *wanted* them to know the memory of its ruin, of its murder, pulled the strings. It, along with something else. The rot festering in the wound. "This place and Hush."

"Is that the name by which she now goes?"

They started, eyed the master of the voice as he approached. He looked every bit of Alerion, midnight-feathered wings and all, but Avaria knew he was not. He reeked of guilt, of anguish. Of pained intent.

"If by she, you mean Mirkvahíl, then yes," Avaria said.

The man eyed him unblinkingly. His stare was glossy, as if Avaria had roused a memory. The man approached; he towered over Avaria, cupped his face and stared into his eyes. "I knew it…" he whispered. "Eyes never lie. Jor Dov'an, as I live and breathe."

He embraced Avaria, clutched him to his chest as if he might fade from existence otherwise.

Avaria returned the gesture; for half a second, it was as if he were home. Varésh Lúm-talé—the name by which this man had gone—had been an uncle to Avaria—Jor—whilst growing up in Ouran'an. A storyteller and a conjurer of possibilities and dreams. He had instilled in Jor the certainty that one day he would see the world beyond the walls of Ouran'an.

Oh, how right he had been.

They pulled away from each other.

Erath looked somewhere in between confusion, exhaustion, and acceptance of the fact that nothing made sense anymore. Sense had all but died the day Avaria departed Helveden.

"Here we stand," murmured Varésh. "In the heart of guilt. So much weight…" He eyed Avaria and Erath. "A man who has cheated time and a woman harboring a power none have ever used for good." He touched his temple at Erath's frown. "The Nameless are afflicted with the memories of every retched life that we have lived. Such is the way of the illum network."

"I pulled this one"—Erath nodded at Avaria—"from the edge of oblivion. That must be a start toward something good, right? To balance. I think."

Varésh touched her cheek. Nodded. "Balance is evasive. Sought by many, found by few. But you..." Erath's flesh bloomed with rivulets of gentle light. "Something in you wakes."

Gods. What was it with gods and oracular statements? Avaria arched an eyebrow. "Something being...?"

Varésh shrugged. Typical. "Left to hatch as time wills."

"What now?" Erath asked.

"We follow our guilt," said Varésh.

To the heart of Banerowos.

The genesis of mad worlds.

"TIME," MUSED THE black-eyed woman. "A beautiful name."

Her smile fell.

"What ails you?" Time asked.

"Many things," she whispered, and her torment spilled from trembling lips.

"I see," said Time. "You are dying in your world."

She was so young. Did he dare?

"What is your power for if not to keep the balance?" a voice inside him asked.

"Some things," said a second voice, *"ought not be meddled in."*

Time gazed at the young woman. Bore into her abyssal stare and dreamt her pain. She was fading. Her world waned. An important one. It whispered in his mind.

He withdrew his stare.

"Fool," the second voice hissed.

"There is a way," said Time. "Words have power."

THE TREE IN the center of Sleep was the last to fall.

Time bowed his head to the pile of ash and wept.

Yowled. Fell to the dead grass graced with the corpses of a million stars, a million dreams, and writhed. Shrieked. Retched. This was what it felt like to be sundered from the inside out. So cold he felt aflame.

"You fool," that distant second voice hissed, wept. *"You ut-*

ter fool."

Time was still. What a fool, indeed.

Silence so profound he could hear the shrieks of all whom he had failed.

Darkness.

"Hell is a place of one's own making."

Had he said that?

Blink.

The gloom of the world bloomed like fire in grass.

Geph gasped. Sputtered.

Sobbed.

Pandemonium

When had they arrived?

How long had they been here?

Fenrin groaned. Blinked, took in the ugly gray. So many holes in his memories. Not the first time that had happened, not that he was a fan of such obscurity.

He forced himself to stand, nearly stumbled forward thanks to legs weighted by disuse. Truly, how long they been here? They. Them. Kept thinking in pluralities. Looked about—no Luminíl. Just a gorgeous nightmare wrought from darkness, flame, and the light of countless dead and dying stars.

Fear compelled his tongue.

"Are you the one called Hush?"

"In a manner." A voice like dry leaves on an autumn wind.

Elseworlds and effigies snapped across his mind. Memories not his own.

"I see," said Fenrin. He feared this thing, yet his heart ached for her. "Mirkvahíl."

"I never left," she murmured. "Not entirely. This place is cruel... *I* am cruel."

Fenrin clenched his teeth, pushed fruitlessly against the unseen force that brought him to knees. Mirkvahíl was still, eyed him with that horrible starlit gaze. Tattered wings fluttered sadly in the breeze. "You should not have come, Wolf King. I will ruin you." A ragged sigh. "I do not want to—but I will."

Distant shrieks. Disembodied, trapped beyond a veil. Fenrin swallowed a howl.

Mirkvahíl turned, paced slowly, wings trailing like the train of a dress. "...I never wanted *any* of this. Fool... what a fool, I was." She cackled. The tower—Fenrin saw now they were at the pinnacle of a tower—trembled. The cackling fell to a deep sob. "What a fool..."

"You have agency over your actions," Fenrin said. Gasped at the release of weight and rose to his full height. "Why not end this?"

She shook her head. "You know nothing..." Drew a ragged breath, exhaled; the city wailed. "And you know not of what you ask." She tilted her head. "Can you hear it, Wolf King? Can you hear them cry? They are hungry—and they are here."

That ugly voice in his head.

"Rend. Rip. Repeat."

Their anguish as he tore them limb from limb.

"Blood. Blood for the gods of old."

Such fountains of exaltation.

Fenrin closed his eyes. The monster in the darkness met his stare.

"Guilt is mighty," it said. *"I knew one day you would come."*

Memories of a world beyond, of a tree and a town that once had been.

I will be the Dream Wolf once again, he whispered. *Such little nightmares will I eat.*

The corpse of Banerowos bloomed before his eyes. Fenrin howled, the ruin shook. He flexed his muscles, twitched his tail; this felt right.

He took a running start and leapt.

HUSH WHIMPERS IN the cold and dark of Hang-Dead Forest. Retches at the memories stoked by whispers from the bodies that the trees once wore like festive bells.

"*The veil is weak here.*" Hush starts at the voice. Whirls around. An iteration of her lovely Luminíl. A phantom from a dream. Her name is Djen. "*Nightmares touch what once they could not.*"

"I did this," whispers Hush.

"*Hell is a place of one's own making,*" Djen says.

Hush shivers. She has lost count of how many times that phrase has scraped across her mind like a rusted blade.

"*Why have you come?*" Djen asks. "*What more could you possibly do? How many more ways must I suffer at your hands?*"

"No more suffering. I can fix this," Hush says. "I *will.*"

Djen snorts. "*You* won't, *because you never do. You only ever make things worse.*" She pointed beyond the trees. "*The culmination of your recklessness and arrogance stands atop the spire at the center of the city. You will destroy it—*her*—if you truly mean to make amends.*"

She sighs. Shakes her head. Her eyes are soft, sad. "*Look at you, my love. This monster you've become. So far gone you have to wear another's face.*" She reaches for Hush, brushes her cheek. "*My Rhona.*"

Rhona.

The forest wanes and waxes, slips in and out of dreams; corpses swing from trees in a pendulum dance and Rhona leads her quarry through the gloom by a tether 'round her neck.

"I do as the Raven wills," she murmurs, and she knows it's all a lie.

She is a lie.

The forest dilates into darkness.

A man screams.

"WE ARE ALL *of us puppets*," Mirkvahíl uttered. She tugged on Hush's soul from atop the spire. Heard a man scream. "*I'm destroying me, my Luminíl. Colliding worlds will set you free.*"

She walked to the edge of the spire and jumped.

How many times was a man destined to see his mother's death?

As Avaria, Queen Ahnil.

As Jor Dov'an, Aveline and Hush.

So wicked was the world that he should lose his mother thrice. He cradled Aveline Dov'an, the monstress wearing her at least. Hush, who'd found him in the rocks and snow near

Ouran'an, who had raised him as her own.

She touched his cheek with a cold hand. "…My Jor." Two voices. Avaria choked back a sob. All this time, Aveline had lived. "My boy…"

"You have to rest," Avaria said. "I…"

Fuck.

Fuck.

"So many sins," she whimpered; there was a wholeness to her voice, one that Hush had always lacked. She looked at Geph, at Erath. "I never wanted"—she coughed blood—"this. I did not want to murder them—but I did. Colliding worlds make monsters of us all."

Her flesh peeled like dry paper in the breeze. Threads of mirkúr twisted from the cracks. Braided, swam like serpents toward the center of Banerowos.

"Please… kill me."

And he was holding ash where once had been his mother.

THE REMNANTS OF Hush's essence brushed Erath as they were drawn away. Kissed her flesh, her mind, and she understood what Hush had meant about having not meant to murder "them."

Aveline. And…

Her knees trembled; it was all she could do to keep from dropping to the earth.

Silith, Queen of the Drenarians, was dead.

Her *mother* was dead.

"WE HAVE TO end this," said Geph. He could smell the woe on Avaria and Erath. The remorse on Varésh Lúm-talé. This was enough. At its root, this broken world was his creation. He had given Mirkvahíl the keys to monstrousness. Had let her taint and twist a million times a million worlds with her toxic desperation. "Before it's too late."

Maybe it already was.

He yelped, whimpered as the temperature fell. So cold. Such anguish. Only the Vulture had ever touched him with such ice.

She approached at a measured pace, trailing tattered wings, eyes like flame and dying stars. "Welcome home," she said with a voice like dry leaves on the wind. "All of you—so pleased I am to see you here. So long it's been since last I felt your woe."

Gods but there was madness in those eyes.

"We can change things, you and I. Rewrite history to right our wrongs. Return to us the ones we left behind. So special, each of you…"

Avaria, who had leapt through time with every death.

Varésh Lúm-talé, who had swum the Temporal Sea.

Erath, wielder of radich.

And Geph, the previous personification of Time.

"You knew," he uttered, more to himself than Mirkvahíl. "You knew trauma would draw us here—you strung us up like puppets." He snarled at the Vulture. "I helped you once and you destroyed my world. I helped you, and you betrayed your Luminíl."

They encircled Mirkvahíl; Geph felt their rage, *fed* of it. So pure. So hot. *True sin, Gephorax. True sin.* Wrath to strike the monstress down. Wrath to save the world.

"EVEN NOW YOU hide. Even now you lie to yourself," said Luminíl. "And for what? Are you so afraid to face the weapons you have wrought? Are you coward enough you cannot look them in the eyes—the lives of whom you robbed of mothers?"

Mirkvahíl whirled to face her. What a sorry thing she had become. Little less than a remnant of the woman Luminíl had loved those millennia ago when the world was new.

"Underlight is a peculiar place," continued Luminíl. "Labyrinthine, yes, but offering clarity for that is how places of its nature work. These... Pockets of Arcadia as they're known. Do you know what I saw?" She stepped toward Mirkvahíl. "Failure. Dead worlds. You cannot fix what you have wrought, dear Mirkvahíl, because that point in time is lost."

"You lie," said Mirkvahíl. The wind howled; battle sang. So much agony in those ruined streets below. "You are my guilt come to sway me from my prize. *I can fix this!*"

Tentacles of shadow fanned from Mirkvahíl; Luminíl deflected them with ease. The Vulture lacked focus and so unknowingly bled strength.

"I can save you, Luminíl. I can save us!"

Us. Them.

Luminíl sighed. "We ended long ago, my Mirkvahíl. And when this night is done, either one or both of us will be a memory."

She unfurled her great, feathered wings and launched herself at Mirkvahíl, but there was only mist. It descended, melded with the spire.

"Have it your way," Luminíl said, and she leapt, hurtling

into chaos.

AVARIA SWUNG MIRKÚR blades at Mirkvahíl, but the Vulture moved too quickly to be hit. He stumbled, barely managing to evade retaliation as a spear of darkness screamed past his ear.

"You are swinging far too wildly," chided Jor. *"Do you remember nothing? Balance is the key. You cannot bend beneath the madness of this thing."*

That was easier said than done for Mirkvahíl exuded frenzied rage. Desperation. She was a parasite of woe infecting all within proximity of her rot.

Avaria rolled behind a slab of ruin. *What do you suggest?*

"Trick her."

How the fuck was he supposed to do that?

He peeked around the debris, watched tendrils of myriad hue and luminosity twist and javelin through the air. Watched Geph and Erath dance as best they could. Heard the shrieks and howls of nearing beasts.

Watched Varésh run the Vulture through with a mirkúr blade and—

Cold air and the kiss of darkness. A throng of distant whispers in his ears.

His eyes adjusted; he was in the bowels of the spire.

VARÉSH LÚM-TALÉ›S PEOPLE called this place the Temporal Annex. He called it his last resort. Jor Dov›an was dead, and this time the old rites wouldn't be enough to bring him back. Something—some things—had to change.

"Are you sure about this?" Erath pulled her cloak tight to ward away the valley wind.

Varésh nodded. "That boy was the closest thing to a son I ever had."

"I understand," Erath said. "I miss him too but consider the consequences."

"I already have."

Varésh stepped toward the stone door embedded in the mossy earth. He knelt and traced the symbols with his index finger, imbuing them with light until the door dilated to reveal a flight of stairs. The pair descended silently into the odorless abyss.

"Tell her," his conscience urged. She deserves to know before you bleed her dry.

And she will, Varésh promised. Just before.

His conscience sighed. *"When did you become so lost? The*

you of yesteryear would not have once considered something so extreme. The old you frowned upon such blatant use of temporal alteration. What changed?"

My heart. He understood now, after all these years, the bond between creator and creation. Planets and people were so much more than playthings, momentary means to entertainment. *All of this, all of them… they were my children—*

"And you have not yet erred so monstrously to warrant going through with what you plan," his conscience argued. *"There is something to be said for that. No parent is perfect, Varésh Lúm-talé, but compared to your fellow Architects you have more heart, more compassion in your index finger than they do combined."*

Varésh offered the argument a melancholy smile. *If only that were so. I'm afraid you have confused my ignorance for moderately sound judgement.* He banished the voice to the abyss of his mind and continued his descent.

Erath cleared her throat. "Do these stairs ever end?"

"Eventually," Varésh said. "Though I can't remember when, exactly."

"Hmm." She rapped the hilt of her dagger. "This place is what…?"

"Far beyond your comprehension, cherished female."

Varésh could practically feel her glare. "Beyond anyone's, really. Imagine, if you can, the absence of time, or yourself existing independently of time."

Erath was silent as the stairway bottomed out into an anteroom of polished white stone. She offered nothing save a deadpan stare and Varésh could tell that she was flummoxed. Or, at the very least, highly annoyed. So, he grinned.

Erath glared. "Could you at least tell me where on Harthe we are?"

"I could," Varésh said, "but it would be irrelevant. We aren't anywhere. Or perhaps we're everywhere. It really is hard to keep it all straight." He wrinkled his nose and blew a strand of dark hair out of his eyes. "Call it… an island somewhere in the Temporal Sea."

Her glared persisted. "Sometimes I really want to stab you."

Varésh chuckled and kept on across the room. "You and many others, cherished female."

He had gone little more than halfway before an inky mottling bloomed along the walls. It spread like flames through grass, forsaking heat in favor of the ether's biting chill.

And then it was gone.

Varésh blinked and looked about the room.

"Varésh? Are you okay?" Erath jabbed his ribs.

He brushed her hand away, still scanning. "…Yes."

Erath arched an eyebrow. "Lead the way."

They crossed the threshold to the passageway beyond, its length pervaded by the scent of rain, its domed ceiling dusted endlessly by dots of light. "Each one, an instance," Varésh said. "A second or a year. A millisecond or one thousand years. Every measure of time the mind can comprehend is represented there."

"And those are every instance of time?" Erath asked.

Varésh chuckled. "Hardly a fraction."

The passageway serpentined; the instances multiplied. Varésh's heart thumped, and his palms were sweaty. *You've come this far,* he urged himself. *Commit, or else your journey here was all for naught. Or else Jor Dov'an remains a ghost, a memory lost to time.*

They kept on in silence.

"Has it occurred to you," his conscience said, *"that something here is wrong? See the frost and rot the walls and ceiling bear. See it suffocate the instances; see the memories die. You have brought a poison to this place."*

Varésh scanned the passageway, and all was well.

The only poison I have brought, he said, *is my intent to bleed this woman dry.*

His conscience growled. *"So, I'm the problem here?"*

The poison, yes, Varésh thought. *If I weren't so ridden with guilt—*

"Then you would sense the foulness creeping through this place like water permeates the earth," his conscience spat.

"Varésh." Erath's hand upon his shoulder startled him from thought. "You're spacing out again."

Varésh chewed his lip. "Just… overwhelmed." He sighed when his conscience made no attempt to refute his claim. "This place and the weight of its… its everything. It can be a bit much sometimes, which is why I endeavor to frequent the Annex as little as I can. I…"

Varésh trailed off. The weight. The rule: no mortal-born may set foot outside time. He eyed Erath; conjured his blade and placed its length between them. "What is this place?"

Erath held her hands up. "The Temporal Annex. Varésh…?"

He shook his head. "If that were so then the laws of time-lessness would have ripped you to bits." He advanced, the glow of his blade reflecting in Erath's eyes—her black eyes.

"Who are you? Think carefully before you answer, lest I divorce your head and neck."

Erath sighed, and with her sigh came rime and rot and blackness. The Annex dissolved into a city ruin, Erath into a black-eyed silhouette of rage and woe. *"You have no name,"* she rasped. Grabbed his blade. *"You are a lie, and so you are mine."*

Darkness spread in webs beneath his flesh. His illum blade decayed to ash. He wheeled about and started toward a hound and a dagger-wielding woman, each footstep leaving threads of shadow its wake.

Each footstep conjuring the distant cackle-weep of Sonja's ghost.

THE INTERIOR OF the spire was dark, save for the small threads of gray light seeping through the cracks. The floor was stone with varying spherical designs. On either side were columns, running all the way to the end of the room. The density of the walls all but kept the sounds of chaos out, and that meant his own screams would go unheard without.

The darkness here is stifling, Avaria thought. More powerful and ravenous than anything he'd ever felt. He could hear them in his head, whispers. They spoke gibberish at first, but it quickly turned to cackling, and that cackling became a ram, bludgeoning the barriers of his mind. Norema's headless corpse. His mother's face, clear as day, that mad grin stretching nearly ear to her, eyes white as snow.

It was only when Avaria momentarily pushed the images from his mind he realized he was trapped inside the darkness with no light to guide him out. The cackling returned, this time intermixed with childish giggling and the intermittent spoken word.

"*If I am dead upon your reading this…*" the words began. The laughter echoed and Avaria heaved, spewing bile. "*Then know that I thought constantly of you. Know that I am watching over you and am proud of who you have become.*"

"You monster," Avaria growled through his tears.

"*…are arrogant at times…*" There was volume to the cackling now, a physicality that had not been present. "*…I have come to find that people with such glaring faults are often the best…*"

Avaria could not banish her twisted visage from his mind. "STOP IT! STOP IT!" He sprinted blindly, boots smacking stone. He could feel his illum waning; could feel the sin-hounds Envy, Pride, and Wrath, his mirkúr swelling like a coastal storm, and he did not care.

"...I know who you are; I know who you can become. Never be anyone but you.

All my love—"

Avaria shrieked, swinging wildly, blindly, with his blade.

"—*Mother*," the voice finished, howling. The blackness swirled, swayed by a gust of wind. It retracted into itself and swarmed to its origin—the outstretched gauntlet of a thing of smoke and flame, the figure from his dream those months ago.

His shadow.

"You have to admit, that was a damn good trick. It makes this little meeting of ours that much sweeter, would you not agree? I told you she would set us free." It breathed a ragged sigh of ecstasy. "You've no idea how long I've been asleep here, waiting. Mother kept us fed"—it licked its cracked lips—"but nothing beats the real thing. Nothing tastes better than slow-cooked self-loathing."

Avaria roared, lunging forward, but his strike was turned aside with the flick of a wrist. The counter floored Avaria, the force knocking the wind from his lungs. He pushed himself to his feet and leapt again, turned away once more, a mocking laughter bouncing off the walls.

"Fight me, you fuck!" Avaria snarled, wiping blood from his nose.

"So soon?" his shadow asked. "Not until you've heard how much Ahnil screamed inside her mind, how much she begged for mercy as Norema slid her blade into her flesh. Have you ever heard a woman die, Avaria Norrith?"

Avaria swung feebly, too blinded by his rage and tears, to land a hit. The shadow sidestepped easily; Avaria lurched and hit the stones, curled into a ball of misery. The shadow kicked him in the face, shattering several teeth and splitting his lip as its sabaton dragged across Avaria's mouth. Avaria spat blood and fragments, dazed, his vision threatening to fail. With the ounce of willpower that he hadn't yet been robbed of, Avaria forced himself to his feet and conjured his blade again.

The shadow grinned.

Avaria rushed.

AVARIA HIT THE stones again, spitting blood. A couple of ribs were broken, something in his leg had fractured, but he forced himself to stand, to face this monster, the worst of himself. He brought his blade up, feebly deflecting the shadow's strike. It missed his chest by inches, instead screaming down his left arm. Hot pain bloomed almost immediately. There was no conversing with this creature any longer. Whatever joy it had taken in taunting him had vanished. He had to end this quickly.

Avaria dodged another blow. With every swing of that sword, the shadow's attacks gained speed and momentum. It roared, slamming a gauntleted fist into Avaria's chest. Avaria tapped his mirkúr, stepping through the shadows. He emerged on the far side of the chamber, winded. Hadn't done *that* in ages.

Like smoke, the monster was before him. It gripped Avaria by the throat and tossed him like a rag doll, but Avaria rushed again. He vaulted through the shadows, barreling shoulder-first into his demon twin. His right hand found purchase on its armor. Instinctively, Avaria imbued the plate with illum until it shattered like glass.

"You are a Reshaper," Jor urged mentally *"You have all the power you require."*

Avaria grasped at the breastplate. The shadow, though, had caught on to his plan. Face contorted with rage, it lashed out with a series of furious strikes, drawing crimson grins on Avaria's arms and face.

"Again," Jor said. *"Illum is the key. Balance."*

Balance—that was it. The shadow was conflicted, off kilter. So much mirkúr, so little illum.

"Come here, you fuck," he growled. He had to end this thing.

He had an idea to weaken Mirkvahíl.

HOW SWEET THEY tasted. How divine their deaths in a ruin long condemned to rot. He had eaten each and every one as they arrived. Every wrong and twisted soul, hound and Jémoonite alike. Devoured and delivered from millennia of hell. All save one. Pale-eyed, dead of flesh, hair trailing to mist.

"Sonja," he said. Such horror. "You seek vengeance."

"No," she hissed. *"Catharsis."*

Her fingers were talons, her memories were black, a master of the pendulum dance. A partnerless waltz in the dark of the wood.

"He will falter," she said. *"As he is fated. He is nameless yet he is also a lie."* Her eyes shone. *"They both are lies. He and the Vulture up high. But I know where she sleeps; I know where she hides."*

Fenrin lowered himself; Sonja climbed onto his back.

"In the heart of the tallest tower stands a tree."

AVARIA HAD DISAPPEARED. It was all Geph and Erath could do to push back against Mirkvahíl and her puppet. Varésh Lúm-talé had fallen prey to her rotten touch. Rather, he had fallen prey to himself, and the Vulture had done what carrion creatures do best.

He lunged at Geph with that dark blade, propelled with a flap of his wings. Geph leapt to the side. Where he'd stood, where the blade made contact, was ash. Whatever it was the Vulture had done to Varésh Lúm-talé had turned him into wither made manifest.

He vaulted toward Geph again, using his wings to add strength to his strike. Geph faltered—but the blade was turned back a sword of brilliant blue light. Erath pushed against Varésh, her flesh alight with radich. She swung with the prowess of a seasoned warrior, and each strike seemed to slow Varésh's moves.

Geph shifted focus to the Vulture. Bared his teeth and closed the distance between them with a single leap. He clamped his jaws around her shoulder and shook, tasting the sour sick of the fluid oozing from the wound. He dug in, bore his claws into her side; fed on the wrath of countless dead as he mangled her arm.

She flung him back with a shriek; Geph landed on his feet.

"I made you," he growled. "I will end you."

Something snapped, popped in the center of his mind and he could perceive time as sharp fluctuations of temperature. So frigid was the past, so seething was the present. He danced the temporal current; waltzed between the golden years and corpse of Banerowos as he zeroed in on the Vulture. She had been beautiful once—a thousand times over, in fact. But he had made her *this*. Abetted insanity.

He emerged from the current in a blur, barreling into her with the weight of a thousand years behind him—but she was smoke. Geph plunged into the temporal current, searching.

Something smelled wrong.

ERATH PARRIED, DROVE her blade into Varésh all the way to the hilt. The moment stilled; the world fluctuated; memories shifted. So many failures; so many desperate iterations doomed to fail. How could they not have seen? How could they wield such energy as radich yet be ignorant of the past? So much possibility, so little wisdom.

She yanked the blade from his chest with a squelch and he fell to his knees.

"Such… hell," he murmured, tears trailing down his cracked cheeks. "What a lie." He met her eyes. "We never deserved such power, did my temporal twins and I. Power… does terrible things." He titled his head back to look at the ugly night. "I thought I was a god… but I was only a fool."

Gradually, he wilted, and his body fell to ash.

"You *all* are fools," Erath whispered of his iterations. "And you will never learn."

Time was not a thing to be meddled with. She lamented their arrogance—theirs and Aveline's. Mirkvahíl's, even, curse the wretched beast.

Erath looked about; she was alone.

She started for the center of the city at a run.

House of the Dying Sun

A varia lunged at his shadow, grasping desperately at the plate carapace it wore. If he could just shatter that armor and reach the flesh it concealed...

"Every move. Futile." The shadow caught him with an elbow to the throat.

Avaria spat blood. His muscles ached; his bones screamed. He could hardly find the strength to move. What small amount he still possessed served little more than to allow the shadow a shot at his face. The sabaton connected with a crunch.

"This?" It stomped again. "Fun. Simple sport."

"Reshape," Avaria gurgled. His vision was clouded, speech partially obstructed by a broken nose. He spat more blood, fragments of teeth. "Remake." He coughed. "Fix... the past."

"Mother has already begun," the shadow hissed, sword raised above its head.

Avaria could hardly move.

A burst of illumination rippled through the chamber and speared the shadow in the chest. It hit the wall with a crack, sword knocked from its grasp.

Through the growing haze, Avaria saw two figures charge the room. Both female from the looks, though it was hard to make out much except the fact that one looked dead and the other gripped a blade of brilliance unlike anything Avaria had ever seen.

"DAMN IT ALL," Erath cursed. She knelt beside Avaria's mangled... Fuck, she hoped 'corpse' wasn't the right word. Not now. Not when mad-as-shit goddesses saw fit to send the world to its end.

"Avaria Norrith... Jor Dov'an—whoever the fuck you are—you had best open your eyes." She touched a glowing fingertip to his chest. "A little pain never hurt, hmm?"

Avaria gurgled. Then came a word. Or was it a name?

Erath frowned. "What was that? Ee? What the hell does that mean?" She leaned in closer; her eyes widened. "*Me—you.*" She looked up, wincing as Sonja—her new companion—took a forearm to the chin. Shadows of self had such violent tendencies.

Erath stood and danced her way into the fray, she and Sonja trading blows with Avaria's shadow, memories rushing to the forefront with every swing. Erath's sword screamed down the breastplate. She pushed, urging the radich to leave her blade, to saturate the plate. It was something that had simply come to her on her sprint through Banerowos. If she could imbue these monsters with enough counter energy to achieve balance, there was a chance she could restore their minds.

At least enough to avert disaster. She punched the shadow in the face, grasped its gorget and took an elbow to the eye.

"*Play nicely,*" Sonja hissed. "*Your* true mother *abhorred such violence.*"

That touched a nerve.

The shadow staggered, caught off guard by Sonja's jibe. Erath took the opening and gripped the breastplate and left pauldron, imbuing it with radich. A loud crack sounded as the tarnished plate shattered in several areas.

"How haunted you must be," Erath hissed. "I wonder if you know—"

The shadow snarled. It charged recklessly, blade striking stone as Erath and Sonja parried.

"—that your beloved Mother Mirkvahíl murdered your *true mother*, Aveline." What a shit thing to say. Erath ducked—she was surprised by her newfound agility—and swiped at the shadow's legs. Her sword crashed against the demon's greaves, tripping it. "How many times now has your mother died? And to think—this time you're to blame."

The shadow rolled over, exposed by the fractured plate—an invitation.

Sonja leapt at the opportunity; Erath cried out.

LUMINÍL ENTERED THE central spire. The moment she crossed the threshold she knew that something was wrong. Old energy waned. Old life, old memories. She had seen the girl Erath and the rusalk Sonja enter not minutes ago.

She crossed the antechamber, the density of this ancient spire once more silencing the madness without. Presently, she reached the central chamber. No Erath. No whatever it was they had been fighting.

Her breath caught—Avaria, still as death. Just beyond him, Sonja, writhing. Luminíl crossed the room, dropped to her knees beside the rusalk, lungs tight in her chest.

"Sonja," she whispered.

Sonja groaned, hardly able to sit up. Luminíl conjured an illum wisp and set about analyzing the severity of the rusalk's wounds. She could make out the deep gash in her chest. It hissed and smoked where she had been run through.

"Just a little longer." She pinched the flesh together with one hand, dragging an illuminated fingertip across it with the other as Sonja hissed. It was temporary; Luminíl knew it wouldn't hold. And maybe that was for the best. Maybe Sonja could finally rest.

The tower quaked. Sonja managed to sit herself up, though she looked ready to pass out at any moment. She pointed... Was it up, maybe toward the doorway—outside? Further in?

"*Illum*," she whispered raggedly, spitting blood. "*You have... to flood them.*"

She fell back and her eyes fell shut.

"How many times," Luminíl whispered, "must we suffer for their sins?" She kissed Sonja on the forehead. Her oldest friend, the two of them betrayed. "Rest now. You are free."

Behind her, Avaria groaned. She rushed to his side.

"D-Down," he stammered. He looked beaten to a pulp, yet still he persevered. She pulled him to his feet. "They went... down."

Luminíl's ears twitched. She turned, greeted by Geph and Fenrin. Such auras.

Fenrin eyed Sonja. He bowed his head. "May she finally rest."

"We need to end this," Geph said. "Banerowos is unstable. The more energy Mirkvahíl exerts, the more the city shifts between the veil of time. Whatever it is she's done, whatever monsters she's created, it's quite literally deteriorating the temporal barrier."

"Into the depths," Fenrin said, "for in the heart of the tower stands a tree."

Luminíl sneered. She knew that tree well.

"What a twisted puzzle," Avaria murmured. "It's not that she's deteriorating the temporal barrier. Her mind is labyrinthine, and we are simply pawns." He spat blood. Frowned. "No. Not pawns, I think. Predators—and she is our prey. She is afraid and she runs just as she's always done. Reality bleeds with her internal fictions."

He eyed Sonja's corpse; worry fell over him. "I saw another enter. Was it Erath? Where is she?"

"WHAT DO YOU *fear*?" the darkness asked. "Whom *do you*

fear?"

Daylight and a blazing sun. *"For what do you long?"*

"For that which you desire most, what price will you pay?"
Laughter. A meadow in fall. *"For* whom *you desire most, what price will you pay?"*

A fluttering of wings. Distant screams.

"Stay away," the darkness wept. *"Stay away from this awful place."*

Erath's footfalls echoed; she was in a hallway somewhere, seeking something wrong. Faded symbols lined the walls; the air smelled of a dying breath. The odor dragged her onward, deeper; spellbound, she descended into screams and snaps of falsities. Nightmares lived repeatedly of their master's own volition.

Radich bloomed at the center of her chest, emanating outward as an aegis. Chaos ricocheted off the gentle light as Erath walked, fruitless in its efforts to abscond with her lucidity.

Her descent yawned into a forest dark. Corpses hung from trees and held each other in a dance. Had it not been so macabre, there might have been a beauty to it all. A twisted elegance.

"Are you going to show yourself?" she inquired of the

shadow she had chased. "Or are you going to hide? What a coward, hiding while I stalk your mother's tortured dreams." She had sensed upon entering this place that it defied reality, that somehow Mirkvahíl's insanity was so profound it had infected Banerowos like an incubus, subjecting all to the Vulture's guilt and dread.

Silence.

"You will," she pressed. "Because you don't exist, not entirely. Another lie." Her barrier bloomed. "How many, Mirkvahíl? How many lies do you hide behind? Will you not show yourself to me?"

"You have to know where to look." Luminíl emerged from a twist of light. "She'll not willingly reveal herself to anyone, not even me—but I know where she sleeps. After all this time."

A TREE STOOD near a lake. Neither was an approximation of reality, but an amalgamation of what had been so long ago when the world was good. Rhona slept against its trunk and the wind kissed her cheeks. She could stay here forever. She *would* stay here forever. At least here she was safe; at least here *they* were safe from *her.*

How many horrors had she wrought? Mirkvahíl and Hush. So many more devoid of names and ripe with pain.

"How do you know you're even real?" the voice inside her asked. *"How do you know you're not the lie?"*

Truth be told she didn't. All she knew was she was mad, and the world was dead.

"It didn't have to be like this," the memory of Alerion said.

"But you chose power over people," said the whole of Banerowos.

"Power over love," said the memory of Djen.

"Lies," said a wolf.

Not a memory. She cowered against the tree at the sight of the incorporeal beast. Eyes like dead stars and a form that trailed to mist. "Than Sor'al, please leave me be."

How did she know that name? Why was this monster here?

"I cannot," said Than Sor'al. "Now that I have found you, Vulture, I cannot. You have taken from me—you have taken from us all." It neared her; dropped beside her like a pup. "You have taken from yourself, and that is the most profound sin of them all." It nuzzled her knee; its nose was cold. "It is time for things to end." It shifted shape; before her stood a man of silver hair and eyes. He held his hand to her. "Will you come with me? Will you let me deliver you from this nightmare?"

She stood, took his hand. Tears streamed from her eyes. "I wish I could." The sanctuary melted and a forest dark of dancing corpses bloomed. "But I cannot, and you were a fool to have come here."

"That's the thing," said Than Sor'al. "I am not here."

CHAINS OF ILLUMINATION bound the Vulture where she stood. Behind her reared a tree that Avaria had seen so many times in memories, dreams, and things of each. The Lost Tree. Memory. Sorrow. Thorn. Bringer, the very illum network itself. Encircling the Vulture were Erath, Luminíl, and Fenrin. It was by chance they had come across the former in this twisted place, and it was by greater chance that Fenrin had been far more than he seemed. Wolf King. The Dream Wolf.

Geph stood beside him, fur like needles, teeth bared. His eyes were restless.

"Hang-Dead Forest was beautiful once," Luminíl said softly. She approached the Vulture, stopped just shy of their noses touching. "You were beautiful once, but you lost yourself somewhere and when." She caressed her cheek. "My Mirkvahíl."

"Rhona," said the Vulture. "I am Rhona. Rhona!"

Luminíl shook her head sadly. "Lies. Even now, at the end."

"Rhona!" she sobbed. "I want... to be Rhona. To *be*—"

In a flash, Rhona fell to luminescent mist. Blades of darkness strafed the trees and Avaria's shadow erupted from the woods, a sick amalgamation of his inner darkness and what essence of the Vulture remained. He parried the blade, but only just, while Luminíl and Fenrin each were felled before they could retaliate.

Geph howled as corpses fell from the trees and rose like ugly puppets. Howled like Avaria had never heard before and all seemed to *slow*. Together they assailed the shambling dead, and from the corner of his eye Avaria saw a blue light wrap itself around his shadow's neck and *pull*.

He wheeled around and reality was all but still.

No, he thought. *I'm just too slow.*

Erath took his shadow into her, bloomed like an eclipse.

What is she—no! There was another way. "*Erath!*"

She shone like a beacon, pulsing with the brilliance of radich.

Time caught Avaria like the raging sea. His ears rang. He stumbled toward her—

but the blade was already buried in her chest.

And she was on her knees and her eyes were wide.

And the world was silent.

Dying hurt far less than Erath had ever anticipated.

Blood leaked from the wound, from her lips. She was cradled in her father's arms. "I had to," she whispered. She looked at Avaria. "There was no other way. Only…" She gestured vaguely at the dagger, at the glow of radich. "Possibility."

"Then you can save yourself," Avaria whispered. Dropped beside her, held her hand. Tears trickled down his cheeks. "Possibility. You—"

She shook her head. She was cold and the world was growing dark. "Doesn't… work like that." Spat blood. "Only one impossible thing… made possible." Lest the cycle never end; lest the Vulture's madness only spread. She touched his hand, smiled. Looked at her father, Fenrin. "Papa…"

It was good to finally call him that again.

Epilogue—To Those Left Behind

One Year Later

Avaria had never been fond of heights, but even he had to admit the world looked brilliant from so high a perch. Geph sat beside him, tongue hanging lazily from his mouth.

"What a long, strange year it's been…"

Avaria thumbed the bundle in his arms; a lump formed in his throat. It was time.

To express what'd taken him a year to figure out.

To finally say goodbye. Tonight, she'd leave him on a breeze.

Tonight, he'd give his mother's remnants to the world.

A wet, ragged sigh escaped Avaria's lips; he cleared his throat.

"Your mother would be proud," said Geph, "and I'm

proud for her."

Avaria twitched a melancholy smile. Not just a strange year, but a busy one at that. He'd swum the Temporal Sea for educational import. With Geph and Fenrin at his side he'd walked the Fountainhead and seen the madness of it all—the beginning and the end.

"How many worlds, Geph—how many worlds beside our own?"

"A fathomless amount," said Geph. "Where do you think we'll end up next?"

"Somewhere with a gentle breeze, I hope—to remind us both of home."

Footsteps.

"I was wondering when you'd show," Avaria said. He'd detected Fenrin in the illum network several minutes prior. "How are you feeling?"

Fenrin spoke no reply as he joined them. He too held a bundle in his hands.

Avaria gave his arm a pat. "They would be proud of you."

Geph nodded.

Fenrin allowed himself a hint of a smile. There was sadness in his silver eyes; there had been for as long as Avaria had known the man. These days it was simply *more*—and Avaria understood.

"We had little of Alor, and nothing of Leru," said Fenrin softly. "That I should have my Erath's ashes brings me warmth in the worst of ways. If only—Silith…" He fell to his knees, tears streaming from his eyes. "I miss my family."

Avaria bowed his head. A memory bloomed.

Moonlight. Virgin snow. The looming Hall and his mother's gentle hand. She'd always said being drafted to the Hall was the best thing that happened to people. Avaria had never understood why until now. The realization made him weep.

She'd wanted him to have a choice. She'd never wanted him to be a slave to familial convention like Avaness and Maryn, never wanted him shackled to this place, to a city and a country glorifying war. She had loved him in the ways she knew how, the ways by which she'd been shown love for all her life—and she had freed him.

Wind.

A breeze. Cold and comforting all at once—the goddess Luminíl.

"Your sorrow drew me here."

Avaria looked at her, bore into her dead-moon eyes. They

held something she had never shown—hesitation. He beckoned Luminíl to join them in the glade. They were not the
only ones to have lost their loved ones in a war, and Luminíl
had lost hers twice.

"You are welcome here," said Fenrin to the Phoenix as he
rose.

"You're a friend whether you like it or not," said Geph.

Luminíl quirked a smile, the first from her Avaria had ever
seen.

"One year," she said. "One year to the day." She heaved a
sigh and the shadows wept. "Is it possible for joy and misery
to be so heavily entwined? We are all of us free from Mirkvahíl, from her pestilence and sway, and yet her spirit seeks
to harrow me with thoughts of better days..."

Avaria gave her hand a gentle squeeze.

"I want to sleep," said Luminíl. "Would you begrudge my
absence?"

"Not at all," Avaria said. Sleep in the context of a goddess
was a very different thing. "You've earned your rest."

Luminíl smiled and pulled Avaria into a tight embrace.
This, he realized, was the true Luminíl; the Phoenix that'd
been buried in the shadows for a thousand years and more,

bound by misery and guilt. Her tension bled away as he held her close; a spark of warmth bloomed above Avaria's heart.

She was gone.

"I hope we see her again," said Geph.

"As do I," said Fenrin. He walked to the edge of the glade, overlooking the world. From his bundle he procured a glowing illum orb. It hovered in his palm as Fenrin drew its light. When he was done, there lingered several smaller beads as bright as, if not brighter than the source from which they'd come.

"They're beautiful," Geph whispered. "*She's* beautiful."

Avaria swallowed the lump in his throat. He'd thought of Erath with increasing frequency these last few months. She'd saved his life—saved *everyone* by letting Mirkvahíl enthrall her form. Would that he could, he'd find a way to bring her back, but the dead were better left to lie.

He and Geph joined Fenrin at the cliff. From his bundle he procured a similar orb, drew its energy until a dozen motes remained. They hovered there above his palm; for a moment he was scared to let them go, for if he did it meant that she was well and truly gone—and how could he accept the finality of such a thing?

"Letting go is always hard," said Jor.

I know, Avaria thought. *I just...*

"Regret what never was," the allhound said. *"Grief has no chronology; there are many stages, many paths walked many times. In grief we* meet *shame, but there is never shame in* grief, *Avaria."*

Avaria nodded. He felt better for the words. Better, yet still afraid of letting go. *But I must.* He sighed deeply and broke his mental tether to the wisps. Beside him, Fenrin did the same.

They stood there and they stared. And when Fenrin finally withdrew, Avaria lingered longer yet with Geph, watching the remnants of his mother and Erath enfold themselves within the winter night and stars. He trembled.

Geph licked his hand. "Do you remember when we met?"

Avaria smiled—and he sat there in that memory of happiness and snow.

Just a boy

and a dog.

ACKNOWLEDGMENTS

This book. My god, this book. I started this novel early in the summer of 2020 while furloughed from by day job due to the pandemic. Initially scheduled for a November 2020 release, that quickly went out the window and I spent the next year and several months slowly scratching away at the project that would be come the bane of my existence. The middle and end of 2020 were terrible for me mentally and emotionally and this book seemed only to exacerbate that.

However, The World Breaker Requiem is also my catharsis. I wrote it as a way to navigate a lot of lingering feelings of guilt and distress related to my mother's death in 2018. Upon completion in October 2021, I broke down in tears in a hot bath in a London hotel; so much weight had been lifted. I am immensely proud of this book. It is my best work.

I usually cast a wide net when talking about my works in progress, but writing The World Breaker Requiem was a relatively intimate experience. I want to thank the following people, in no specific order, from the bottom of my heart: Sarah Chorn, Tom Clews, Ryan Cahill, Justin Gross, Tessa Hastjarjanto, Justin Wallace, Jodie Crump, Nick Borrelli, Thomas Howard Riley, Justine Bergman, and Sara Carothers. I also want to extend a huge thank you and shoutout to my beta readers Bri Sinder, Rowena Andrews, Joshua Newman, Peter Hutchinson, and Mark a.k.a. Fantasy Book Nerd and my phenomenal editor, Victoria Gross.

Lastly, thank you to my readers, who make writing these stories a little less lonely.

If you enjoyed THE WORLD BREAKER REQUIEM please consider leaving a review on Goodreads and Amazon. I would be nowhere without you, the readers! And be sure to subscribe to my newsletter at luketarzian.com to receive updates, exclusive content, and a FREE ebook copy of THE WORLD MAKER PARABLE. Thank you so much!

Lightning Source UK Ltd.
Milton Keynes UK
UKHW012042281221
396314UK00011B/374/J